The RUSHING WIND

A Soul's Journey Through Time, Destiny, and Dragons

Contents

Preface

Know, therefore, that from the greater silence of the night, in the space beyond space I shall return…Forget not that I shall return to you in a little while, in a moment of quiet on the breath of the wind I shall return…Across the oceans of your world and the ice fields of the mountains high, I shall return…Forget not for I am the dragon of your dreams, the rushing wind and the provider of your future…

Prologue

There is someone special for everyone. Sometimes maybe two, three, or four special people come into your life. They can come from different generations, from different times, from different dimensions. They travel across oceans of time and from the depths of heavenly dimensions especially to be with you.

You cannot predict when they will arrive, but when they do, you shall know. On meeting, a bond is set, like the roots holding up a mighty tree or a mountain gazing down on the valley below. Timeless. It was meant to be, this meeting, no matter how long or short, it was meant to be.

Energy is transferred as the connection is made. Soul touches soul. Eyes see eyes. Hearts join together to beat as one in a compassionate and warming rhythm. There is a sort of chemical exchange between the two physical bodies – what some people would say 'love at first sight'. This is both the aura's joining hands and dancing into the light.

You may be awakened to the presence of a soul companion by a look, a dream, a fleeting memory, or just a feeling that can give you that tingling sensation all over. You may be awakened by the touch of hands, a whispered word, a kiss, and your soul is jolted back to life. The heart becomes alive again, breaking free of the empty desert it may have roamed.

The awakening, when it comes, will be like no other feeling experienced. The energy released will be like a volcano exploding, or the waves crashing heavily on the shore.

The connection is never broken, it can sometimes just get lost for a while. A gentle reminder comes on the wind, which reminds you that you are never truly alone. It comes to remind you that you are together always, to the end of time (your perceived measure of time).

As the light started to turn to dark and the evening descended all around, a dragon came. It came on the wind and its force was rushing…

Majestic, powerful, knowledgeable, soul so full and it took me to a place I had never been before – a plane of enlightenment, mystery, and discovery.

This is the story of my dragon and the connection we made together and the journey we took, back in time and past lives. This is the Rushing Wind…

CHAPTER ONE

Arrival

I had gone to bed early that night, the day that had passed had long lost its attraction. The sun was still in the sky, albeit low and dark orange in colour. The chattering of the songbirds was starting to fade as they to sought to find their night's sleeping place on a perch somewhere in a tree in the garden outside. Darkness gathered its cloak and, caressing the earth, started to chase away the last vestiges of sunlight to usher in the velvet black that is night without a moon.

I couldn't sleep. My mind was full of insignificant data, all competing with each other for my attention in the conscious mind. The 'monkey' in the brain was on overload, chattering to itself back and forth, back and forth. I got out of bed and crossed to the window. Looking outside at the evening rural scene unfolding before me, I could see the sky streaked with magnificent colours. Indigo, orange, pink and slate grey hues painted the sky like an artist's canvas. An old oak tree threw shadows across the mowed lawn and, in the distance, I could see the last rays of the sun sparkling on the estuary water.

As twilight wrapped its gentle arms around the world, Venus emerged like a diamond against darkening silk. At first, it appeared as a mere glimmer, a delicate pulse of light barely visible in the fading day. But as shadows lengthened and deepened, its brilliance grew ever stronger, commanding attention in the western sky. While we call it the evening star - a name it has carried through countless generations - Venus is no star at all, but rather our closest planetary neighbour, a world shrouded in mystery and cloud. When it graces our mornings, it becomes the herald of dawn, the morning star that has guided travelers and dreamers since humanity first gazed skyward. This celestial jewel, brighter than any true star in our night sky, has inspired poets and astronomers alike, its dual nature as both evening and morning star weaving through the stories and myths of every culture that has ever turned their eyes to the heavens.

The entire scene was one of peace and quiet as if Mother Nature herself was coaxing the whole planet in front of me to go to sleep, refresh the body and ease the mind.

All seemed to be in order and all was laid out in perfect harmony. Much of this was utterly contrary to where I felt I was in my life at this time. My life seemed to be a chapter of unlinked stories with no golden 'seam' or thread running through to connect what should be my purpose.

The perennial question: What was my purpose in life? I kept on thinking there must be something bigger that I was not grasping that I should be aware of - but what was it? I mused that this was the eternal question that man has faced and questioned himself since he first emerged from the swamp - why am I here? There must be more to life than just 'being' around.

Indeed, our soul returns time and time again, occupying a new 'frame' (the physical body) to bring around new perspectives, new messages for those around us as well as ourselves. But very often, the 'frame' never knows or asks the question, 'what am I doing here?'

One last look at the sky that was almost black now, I started to draw close the curtains. Gazing up at the evening sky, a black wisp caught my eye and then disappeared again. It must have been a cloud. I turned and went back to bed. Resting my head on the pillow I started to drift asleep.

I woke with the sound of cars rushing along the road outside. Their occupants rushing to go to work, to beat the traffic, to get that car space, to enter their habitual world of 9 to 5.

I could not remember if I had dreamed at all. Another night with no insight… something told me that I needed to start talking to my unconscious mind to unravel what lay there below the surface that was bursting to tell me. Buffy's (the love of my life) therapy room downstairs was the place to go. Somewhat lazily I got out of bed, threw some water over my face and walked downstairs.

The small room was a place of sanctuary. As I entered, it felt like going into a different world. The smells of essential oils entered my nostrils. A whiff of lavender and rosemary in one corner, thyme and yan yan in another. Looking around I could see the glint of various crystals and beautifully coloured stones reflecting the light from candles that were lit. Strange coloured posters hung on the walls, quite surreal really, the artists clearly driven by inspiration with which to transfer colour, shape and feeling to the canvass. This was the best place for me to meditate. Here, I could escape the world outside, even just for a few minutes. It was a place of calm, solitude and discovery. I sat in the middle of the room closed my eyes and started to breathe deeply and meditate…

Slowly my mind cleared and calmed. I am walking in a beautiful forest that seemed to be high up in the mountains. The air is deliciously clean, and the only noise is that of the sounds of my footsteps moving along a path. I came across a clearing that gave me the wonderous view to more mountains in the distance and purple lined clouds drifting slowly across the horizon. I became aware of the sound of water and walked towards it. I am now seated comfortably on an enormous guardian rock, a short distance from a high waterfall that sent water down into a deep pool below before flowing further downstream. Tall redwood trees that provide a high canopy and shade surround the river as it flows away from the waterfall pool. The air is cool and comfortable, and a gentle breeze blows through the trunks of the trees around me caressing my face like gentle silk.

Now I can feel all of my frustrations and negative emotions physically in my body. I imagine that they are manifested as a kind of black tar or sludge that has accumulated in different areas all throughout my body, in my bones and in the soft tissues and cells of my body. All my fears, my negative thoughts and feelings, any emotions that I would like to let go of – I can see that these are all trapped within my body - and they are black.

I stay with this feeling for a moment, even though it is a little bit unpleasant and challenging. I have to let go of any resistance to these thoughts or emotions and let them be here in my body. Just for a moment, I have to feel what I feel, accepting that this is truth, this is reality and that I have a choice to reject or to accept. I have the choice; it is only I that can make it.

I try to see whether there is part of me that is grateful for what these negative emotions taught me in the past on my journey to this moment. It's hard, this feeling, but I must surrender to the good and the bad and honour both for the life lessons. I believe this is the only way to grow, to discover, to be.

I now stand up and walk over toward the base of the waterfall. I can feel a faint mist of water hitting my face and strangely, my arms appear to get stronger and stronger as I approach closer.

Just as all my negative emotions are now physically manifested in my body, this waterfall is a physical manifestation of pure Source energy. As I walk under the powerful stream of falling pure water, the purest that the mountain gives to the earth, the water starts to interact with all those emotions and gradually dissolves them. I am now standing tall on a moss covered rock, with my feet firmly anchored on the rough, green mossy surface, and the powerful stream of water is flowing over me and through me.

Now the emotions anchored in my head are dissolving and flowing away, through my body, through the tips of my fingers, out the bottom of my feet and through the ends of my toes.

The emotions, feelings and fears that used to be trapped in my neck and shoulders all dissolve away and flow out through my fingertips and toes and out through the bottoms of my feet and my neck and shoulders feel massaged and cleansed.

Next the water flows through cleansing the negative emotions out of my chest and arms, and all the sludge of emotion is released and flows away. It's easy to cleanse the arms because the emotions just flow straight down, out through my fingertips. The flowing water starts off dark and dirty, and runs cleaner and cleaner until there's no difference between the water entering me and the water flowing out of my fingertips.

Now my entire upper body has been cleansed and the entire force of the waterfall goes to work washing away all the negative emotions contained in my lower body.

The powerful stream of water keeps working lower and lower, eroding all the fears and negative feelings contained in my upper legs, in the quadriceps and hamstring muscles, and breaking up any knots of negative emotion in my knees, and then in my calves, and reaching any sludge left over in my feet.

Finally, I feel the last fragments and droplets of sludge flow out the end of my toes. I feel the water flowing from the top of my head, energizing it and purifying my connection to consciousness itself while opening the door to the sub conscious.

I carefully step out of the powerful flow of falling water and walk back to the place that I started, on the thick carpet of moss a short distance from the waterfall. I am just sitting there with my body supported by this natural green carpet of moss, breathing in the cool and refreshing mountain air.

Something happens, I am not sure what. I feel wonderfully clean, but the questions are still there. I tell myself that I need to do more of this, daily perhaps. The air temperature noticeably starts to rise. The mountain air is no longer crisp and sharp – in fact the mountains seem to be fading. I rub my eyes. Am I still in a meditative state or am I waking up? The heat increases, as does the 'fade' in the scenery around me. I am going somewhere else…

CHAPTER TWO

Encounter

I was wandering in a desert. Nothing moved, nothing could be seen except countless miles and miles of sand. I could 'see' the heat coming off the sand, like shimmering waves going up into the sky. Even though I was surrounded by heat and the sound of silence, I walked along feeling very cool inside my body. I did not feel physically stressed or alarmed at where I was.

Whilst I was thinking and walking, I became aware of a large presence behind me. Probably out of fear I did not turn around - I just kept walking. Then came a voice. A very deep, powerful yet soothing tone said to me "Mike, turn around." I simply could not turn around maybe through trepidation or because I just wanted to keep walking the way I was, without this interruption. The inner voice inside me started to contradict itself, 'yes go on look', 'no don't, 'go on look', 'don't be stupid'... I stopped walking. I could feel my heart beating, and it sounded as loud as a beating drum - surely the whole desert could hear it – the desert could probably smell my fear also. I looked down and saw a wet spot in front of my feet - it started to grow and I realised it was sweat dropping from my head and brow. So, I was hot after all! Seeing the sweat drop stain the sand, broke the spell and suddenly something inside me clicked - I had to turn around and face whatever it was behind me. I was most certainly alive and curiosity drew me to this fear, real or imaginary. After all, we make our own fear, most of it irrational anyway.

I turned.

This precise moment was one of those 'mega' moments that we have in our lives, and we do not have many of them. There, standing in front of me, was a real live dragon. Unbelievable, a dragon for goodness sake!

Its scales were made of malachite crystals, bright green with darker green bands that merged into black under its belly. It had a magnificent gold coloured ridge that ran from the base of its head all the way down to the tail end. The scales were like an armoured suit, so strong and hard looking, yet they appeared to move easily with its slow rhythmic breath. It had a muscular body with long limbs, each supported by five closely mounted claws on feet. Two massive translucent wings drooped heavily on the ground beside it. The head was powerful yet somewhat elongated with a huge mouth displaying plenty of teeth. The most striking thing (if seeing a real dragon was not striking enough!) was its eyes, which glowed the deepest blue like the deep ocean itself. As it spoke, its breath appeared as a thin cloud of misty vapour.

"Where are you going Mike?"

My mind was spinning like a dervish and my physical body was trembling. How, why, what, who…

Finally, I plucked up the courage and asked the dumbest question, "Are you for real? I mean, why are you here and speaking to me?"

The dragon looked at me and cocked its massive head to one side. "Why, I am here for you of course, and yes, I am a very real dragon. I have come to you as part of my destiny, and yours. You have nothing to worry about, even though I can see terror in your face, uncertainty in your mind and fear in your heart. I understand this is a shock for you but be calm and trust."

"I do not understand. I am confused and yes, I am frightened", I blurted back. "I mean, it is not everyday that I meet a mythical animal!"

"Well, that's a wonderful response" said the dragon, "and the first step to enlightenment – being true to yourself. By the way, I am not 'mythical' as you put it. I am just one of many thousand so-called mythical creatures that inhabit your planet, it's just that you do not really SEE us or BELIEVE in us. Therefore you cannot see us. But we are here and always have been. The clues as to who you are and who you are to become, are all locked in your mythology. I will show you the light on this.”

“But why me?” I blurted out.

“Ah, to understand fully, I must tell you about my purpose, my beginnings, my life and in that way you will begin to understand why you are the one that I must guide for your future path and the paths of others. I have been with you for many lifetimes by the way. Here, sit beside me and touch my forehead. This will allow you to ‘see’ and well as hear my story.”

I felt somewhat foolish accepting this offer. Why would I sit down in a desert, touch a dragon to listen and ‘see’ a story? Was I completely mad? Of course, the other part of me was really curious and excited to have this completely weird opportunity.

Funny thing that, how we often refer to ‘part of me’ in conversation? Do you know what I mean? We strike up conversation either with others or indeed with ourselves, and say ‘part of me would like this, but part of me thinks we should do that…’ it is like we have two parts to our mind or body, whereas the reality is of course we only have one brain and thus one mind and one body. However, particular emotional and physical experiences throughout our early life can result in the creation of ‘parts’ in the area of the brain that we call the unconscious mind. These ‘parts’ can generate their own value sets and beliefs, and these can be responsible for certain behaviors. To that end, overwhelming feelings and reactions, as well as out of control behaviors are often the result of ‘conflicting parts’.

So, yes, I was experiencing overwhelming feelings of apprehension, wonderment and curiosity at this invitation to listen to a dragon.

Cautiously, I sat down beside the dragon. The sand should have been burning hot, but it felt like I was sitting on a lush, cool carpet of freshly mown grass. I put out my hand to touch the dragon's skin, and I was in for another surprise. Even though the scales looked hard and tough, they actually felt soft and smooth, a little like moleskin. I ran my hand along the jawline, marveling at the smoothness.

"So, let us begin" the dragon said, "leave your hand on my head, close your eyes and just listen"

"Sorry, before we start, you know my name, but what is yours?"

"My name is Ceres and I have lived for eons, but then again, so have you Mike."

And so started the dragons story:

I was born out of a cosmic egg in the chaotic seas of Nu at the centre of what you would call the cosmos. This centre is everything and nothing, what is and what is not. The constantly changing nature of the sea and the liquid quality of the shifting energetic waters in general, brought about many different forms of life, material and energy clusters. All of these, including my egg, were cast out into the void by a cataclysmic eruption at the cosmic core, which spun everything through the matter of the dark beyond the dark and into new galaxies.

And thus, my life commenced, journeying though the void encased inside my eggshell. The space beyond the space. The magnetic and electric pull of the 7th sun took me into its gentle 'custody'. However, I will return to certain passages of my life as we continue our journey together, but as they span the passage of all time, it is better that we start with my arrival onto your planet.

I came to this planet of yours using a portal from a different universe in a different time. There are many portals into your world, some now closed, some very much still open. Portals are chosen for their energy and 'base' needs. All portals are specific to the task that requires intervention/help (the base need). Almost all of them are situated on your ancient religious sites, which in turn are placed on, what you call, ley lines and energetic concentrations or 'power spots'. These energy concentrations and power spots were formed at the birth of your world from the inner galactic void. Most of them are aligned to star systems in your galaxy, and for me, the star gate to the earthly portal I needed was through what you call the Orion and Sirius systems. This particular earth portal that I needed was (and still is) situated at Karnak in Luxor, Egypt at the temple of Amun-Re.

This temple was dedicated to life, its growth and creation, and for me, it was the most powerful route into your planet for the work I needed to do and the most relevant one for me.

On the winter Solstice in 1275 BC (your construct of time) as the sun rose over the horizon, it cast a beam through a perfectly constructed stone block window which was aligned perfectly again to receive the suns rays at a specific time. As the sunrays kissed the earth, they travelled down the Avenue of Sphinxes, through courtyards, passing guarding obelisks, through halls and inner temples until they reached the Holy of Holies, or the High Room of the Sun as it was called then.

There, for a brief time the sun bathed this inner sanctum with delicious golden light and in doing so activated the portal for my arrival. At exactly 7 minutes past 7 am on the 7th of December in 1275 BC, the transmission from the heart of the cosmos started. A 'corridor' of pulsing energy illuminated the path to your earth and specifically into Karnak, which I then followed. Even though this distance from source to your planet is thousands of light years away, the process takes but milli seconds, or what you would call 'in the blink of an eye'.

On arrival, so as not to frighten the locals, I changed shape. I turned into a human.

I forgot to tell you that I am a shape changer or shifter as some of your kind would like to call it. In simple terms this is the ability to change into the form or shape of a person, or indeed the other way from a human form into an animal form. This allows many of us to move about your societies without being too obvious. For me, as a dragon 85 feet long with a wingspan of 170 feet, I would be more than a little obvious among your people, hence the need to change!

I also have the ability to change into an innate object, such as a rock, a door, a tree or even a grain of sand! There is no limit to my powers in this regard.

I assumed the shape of a scribe and was assigned to you, an Egyptian military man, a General of the highest order – the Commander of the Royal Protection Guard to the Great Pharaoh Ramesses II. You were also the Pharaoh's favourite advisor and spent many hours with him in chambers, discussing future military campaigns, the glory of the dynasty and the wealth of the country. As such you were held in high respect and admiration throughout the land.

You became most prominent at the Battle of Kadesh and afterwards in protecting Moses during the Exedos, of which I wish to speak with you now about…

CHAPTER 3

The Egyptian Experience

Ceres moved position slightly, stretched his mighty wings and then began to tell his story about my life, as it was then, in ancient Egypt nearly four thousand years ago. And what a story it was.

"Back in those days (1275 BC), life was much different to what it is today, not just in Ancient Egypt, but all over the world. In those days, power was everything, and no more so than in Egypt. One could argue that the need for a country or entity to pursue power over its inhabitants and neighbours remains very constant today on your planet!

There was a large variety of jobs in Ancient Egypt. There were bakers, scribes, farmers, priests, doctors, craftsmen, merchants and many more. Jobs were usually inherited from your parents – if your father was a farmer, it would be very likely that you would become a farmer too.

There were not schools like the ones you have today, but ancient Egyptians did have apprenticeships. This meant that many children had jobs or were learning a trade as they matured into adulthood.

You were different though, and after leaving home at the age of thirteen years old, you joined the Army and soon rose in the ranks from a nobody, to an officer. This was in the main due to your complete and utter courage in the face of overwhelming odds. It was though you believed that the gods were protecting you on the battlefield, and that injury and pain would never visit you.

As an example, during the Syrian invasion of 1250 BC, as a high-ranking officer you were asked to lead an attack against the enemy occupying the coastal strip town of Amurru. This you did with strategic success and no amount of personal bravery leading from the front, despite being heavily outnumbered. On at least two occasions you were confronted personally by three or more enemy soldiers, but you went through them like a sharp knife through butter. Your troops were motivated by your bravery and responded accordingly sweeping all in front of them to claim victory. You were unaware that watching your efforts on top of a nearby hill was none other than Ramses II, who had been told of your previous military successes. The Pharaoh was impressed and curious enough to see you in a private audience following the battle, and you both spent the night talking and laughing – a bond of mutual friendship that would last your life had been made.

Very soon, the Pharaoh made you his favourite military bodyguard and promoted you to the exalted rank of General. You now had the admiration and popularity, not only in the royal court, but also among the people in the street who saw you alongside their Pharaoh. Your role was to be alongside the Pharaoh at all times, to protect him from any threat, and to advise him on any matter you felt was appropriate for the Pharaoh to know.

It was in 1275 BC, that Ramses II began a campaign to recover lost provinces further in the north in what is now modern day Syria. The most significant battle of this campaign was the Battle of Kadesh, fought in 1274 BC against the Hittite Empire under Muwatalli II.

It involved around 5,000 to 6,000 chariots, making it perhaps the largest chariot battle ever fought, and both Egyptians and Hittite's fought ferociously. It got so heated that even the young Pharoah was seen on the battlefield with you, his personal protector, side by side, fighting hard. Ramses fought bravely with spear and sword, however he was vastly outnumbered and was caught in an ambush by the Hittite army and narrowly escaped death on the battlefield. He owed his life to you on at least two occasions during those ferocious encounters.

At the moment of truth, and at what seemed to be the critical point of the battle, Ramses II personally led a counterattack to drive the Hittites away from the somewhat overwhelmed main Egyptian army. You fought with him side by side, and while the battle was inconclusive, Ramses emerged as the hero of the hour. The Hittites decided that nothing would come of continued bloodshed and withdrew from the battlefield and took up defensive positions 5 miles away on top of a high ridgeline. Ramses sent you forward as a negotiator with the Hittites and over a period of two days talking, you secured a peace and territory solution that suited the Pharaohs satisfaction. And with that, he promoted you as his vizier for life.

The viziers were appointed directly and only by the Pharaoh. Your paramount duty was to supervise the running of the country. You also supervised the security of the Pharaoh and the palace by overseeing the comings and goings of palace visitors. You would often act as the Pharaoh's seal bearer as well, and on occasions, received other countries representatives on the Pharaoh's behalf.

Within two years of being appointed, you were the highest civilian bureaucratic official and held supreme responsibility for the administration of the palace and government, including jurisdiction, scribes, state archives, central granaries, treasury, storage of surplus products and their redistribution, and supervision of building projects such as the royal pyramid."

As I sat with Ceres, listening to his tale of my past life, memories of ancient Egypt flooded back. My bond with Ramses II was unbreakable, forged in the fires of battle and tempered by mutual respect. Yet, destiny had other plans. The arrival of Moses and the plight of the Israelites stirred something deep within me. Despite my loyalty to the Pharaoh, I felt compelled to aid Moses in his mission to free his people from bondage. It was a decision that tore at my heart, caught between my duty to Ramses and the undeniable call to justice and freedom. The night we left Egypt was filled with tension and uncertainty. As Moses led his people across the Red Sea, I stood by his side, ensuring their safe passage. The cries of joy and relief from the Israelites were bittersweet, for I knew that my actions marked a point of no return.

Our journey took us through harsh deserts and unforgiving landscapes until we reached Mount Sinai. It was there, at the summit, that I watched the sun rise with Moses - a symbol of hope and new beginnings. The golden hues painted across the sky mirrored the promise of liberation for his people.

As the first rays of dawn broke over the horizon, I realised that my path diverged from theirs. I bade farewell to Moses and his followers, knowing they had a new leader to guide them. My heart was heavy yet resolute; I needed to seek my own purpose beyond the shadows of Egypt's grandeur. Leaving them behind, I embarked on a journey of self-discovery, seeking answers to questions that had long haunted me.

What was my true calling? How could I reconcile my past with the future? These questions lingered as I ventured into unknown lands, driven by a desire to understand my place in this vast world and Universe.

Ceres gently folded his wings behind him as he observed me. His gaze was piercing yet kind, as though he could see the weight of the story settling on my shoulders. He continued, his voice resonating with an otherworldly timbre.

"You wandered far beyond the borders of Egypt, through lands that had never known the might of Pharaohs or the whispers of the Nile. Your journey took you to the ancient city of Babylon, where you marveled at the ziggurats that reached toward the heavens and studied under priests who spoke of stars and god's unknown to you. They taught you to read celestial patterns, to see not just the physical world but the threads that wove destiny itself. You became a seeker of knowledge, a student of the cosmos."

"In Babylon, you found yourself drawn to their mysteries - their gods, their sciences, their philosophies. The priests spoke of Ishtar, goddess of love and war, and Marduk, the great protector. Yet even as you immersed yourself in their teachings, you could not escape the memories of Egypt: Ramses' laughter echoing in his golden halls, the cries of battle on the plains of Kadesh, and Moses' unwavering faith as he led his people to freedom. These memories were like ghosts, haunting your every step."

"It was during your time in Babylon that you began to dream - visions so vivid they felt more real than waking life. In these dreams, you saw a great dragon with wings like fire and eyes like molten gold. It spoke to you in a language older than time itself, calling you by a name you had forgotten but which resonated deep within your soul. The dragon told you that your journey was far from over and that your purpose lay not in serving kings or freeing nations but in understanding the balance between power and compassion, between loyalty and justice.

Moved by these visions, you left Babylon and travelled eastward into lands even more mysterious. You crossed treacherous mountains and vast deserts until you reached the Indus Valley. There, among a people who revered rivers as sacred lifelines, you found a new kind of wisdom - one that spoke of inner peace and harmony with nature. The sages there taught you meditation and introspection, helping you confront the duality within yourself: the warrior who had fought for Pharaohs and empires versus the man who had risked everything for freedom and justice.

It was in these moments of reflection that you began to understand your true purpose. You saw that your life had been a tapestry woven from threads of courage, loyalty, love, and sacrifice. Each thread was necessary to create the whole; each experience had shaped you into who you were meant to become. But destiny was not done with you yet.

One fateful night, as you meditated by a river under a canopy of stars, the great dragon from your dreams appeared before you - not as an apparition but in physical form. Its scales shimmered with an ethereal light, and its eyes burned with wisdom beyond comprehension. It introduced itself as Ceres.

"I have watched over you for lifetimes," Ceres said. "You are more than a man; you are an eternal soul bound to this world by a purpose greater than any kingdom or empire. You have walked through fire and shadow to reach this point because only through such trials can one truly understand what it means to be both human and divine."

Ceres revealed that your journey was part of a larger cosmic plan - a cycle of learning and growth that spanned countless lifetimes. In each life, you were given choices: to wield power or to renounce it, to serve others or to serve yourself. Each choice shaped not only your soul but also the world around you.

"You have been a warrior," Ceres continued. "A protector, a liberator, a seeker of truth. But now it is time for you to become something more - a guide for others who are lost in their own journeys."

With Ceres as your companion and mentor, you set out once more - not as a soldier or vizier but as a teacher and healer. You traveled through ancient Persia, Greece, and Rome, sharing your wisdom with those who sought it. You taught kings about humility, warriors about mercy, and scholars about the importance of heart over intellect.

In Greece, you met philosophers like Pythagoras and Socrates, engaging in debates about ethics and existence. In Rome, you advised senators on justice and governance. Everywhere you went, people were drawn to your presence - not because of your past glories but because of the quiet strength and compassion that radiated from within.

As centuries passed, your story became legend - a tale told by firesides about a man who had walked alongside Pharaohs yet chose to walk among commoners; who had fought battles yet sought peace; who had served gods yet sought truth beyond them.

Ceres leaned closer now, his blue eyes locking onto mine. "And so here we are," he said softly. "You have lived many lives since then - each one building upon the last - but this life is special. The world is at a crossroads once again: torn between unity and division, progress and destruction."

He spread his wings wide as if encompassing all of existence within their span.

"You have within you all the wisdom of those past lives - the courage of a warrior-general, the compassion of a liberator, the insight of a seeker. The question is: what will *you* do with it? How will *you* shape this world?»

The weight of his words settled over me like an ancient mantle reclaimed after eons apart. My heart raced as I realised that my journey was far from over - that my purpose was still unfolding.

And so, I asked him: "Where do I begin?"

Ceres smiled - a knowing smile that seemed to hold all the secrets of eternity - and replied simply: "You already have."

CHAPTER 4

Cave Revelations

Without a word, Ceres spread its wings and soared into the sky, taking me clinging onto its back. We flew high above the clouds, past towering mountains and over seemingly vast oceans.

I was doing my best to cling on tightly to the dragon's scales as we soared through the air, my heart pounding with excitement and wonder. It was then that I suddenly felt the confidence just to let go. My mind said, 'be part of Ceres', and so it was. I had no need to hold on to anything – I was part of the spirit of Ceres and thus had no need to cling onto anything. Ceres showed me all the wonders of the world, from hidden waterfalls and secret forests to cities filled with people and animals.

I had no idea how high we were flying, but I guessed it was tens of thousands of feet. It should have been ice cold and blowing a fierce wind strength, but it was like being on a warm beach with a gentle sea breeze gently blowing through my hair.

"Look," said Ceres, "the highest visible mountain range on your planet, the Himalayas."

Flying over the wilderness of the upper Nepal and Bhutan valleys and surrounded by majestic mountain peaks, we came across a large cave entrance. There was something about this rather dark forbidding hole in the side of a cliff that made me nervous, I cannot say why. It was at this point that I resumed my grasp of Ceres - tightly. Without any hesitation, Ceres dipped his left shoulder and quickly flew into the cave opening and the dark.

We stood at the entrance way and looked back out to the far mountain range across the valley. The evening colour sky hues brought about beautiful colours and the showing of a host of emerging stars. The planet Venus was the most obvious brightness in the low sky horizon. Rising in conjunction with Venus was one of the most obvious and recognisable grouping of stars in the night sky. I could see Mintaka, Alnilam and Alnitak twinkling in their familiar row. The majesty of Orion's Belt was all there to be seen rising exactly opposite us in the 'V' shape formed by the valley in between two mountains.

Ceres spoke about the importance of Orion's Belt. He told me that although the grouping was over 1,200 light years from our earth, they had always played a major part in human existence. Indeed, the Ancient Egyptians thought that there is a correlation between the location of the three largest pyramids of the Giza plateau complex and the constellation Orion, and that this correlation was intended as such by the original builders of the Giza pyramid complex. The stars of Orion were associated with Osiris, the god of rebirth and the afterlife by the ancient Egyptians. They also had magical powers for those who sought them.

"These will be your continuing stream of magic in many lives, those 3 magnificent heavenly bodies", he said. "They will return to aid you in times of trouble and be there to guide your perceptions and thoughts to bring good. Indeed, they have often been referred to as a wand in the sky, and it is here in this cave that we will find a gift from Orion's Belt in the shape of a wand. This is why we are here."

We started to move towards what appeared to be a small hole or doorway. Inside, the cave was much larger than I thought it would be. It is dimly lit by glowing crystals that lined the walls and ceiling above. The crystals gave off a warm, soothing light that filled the cave with a soft, ethereal glow.

As we walked deeper into the cave, I started to notice strange symbols and designs etched into the walls. These symbols seem to pulse with a faint, otherworldly energy, and I could not help but feel a sense of awe as I gazed upon them. The other odd thing that struck me, was that these 'etchings' were at least 10 foot off the cave floor. How did they get up there, and why?

"These are the ancient writings", said Ceres quietly, "one day I will explain their meaning to you, but for now, just touch the cave wall."

As I did so, my conscious mind said, "here we go" and then I lost current consciousness. In a dream like state, I saw an old man and woman, dressed in long flowing robes that glowed with a large halo effect around their bodies. There were markings on their robes very much like those I had seen on the cave walls. There was an audible 'buzz' in the air like static electricity. They were pointing at an ancient tree which appeared to be talking to them. The tree had what seemed to be a mouth halfway up its enormous trunk and it was moving.

As the 'mouth' moved so the branches waved about, and the leaves shook. They kept on glancing at me and nodding their heads as if to confirm what the tree was saying.

I felt that I started to connect with the two robed beings by simply just saying to myself repeatedly, "I am listening". Muted unintelligible sounds started to flow across my head in waves like the flow of an oceans swell and entered through my ears. I had no idea what was being said at first, and then I started to hear my name, well, what sounded like my name. This communication seemed to be a series of vocalisations, gestures and even telepathy. This was language 'technology' on a different scale.

I looked carefully at the tree. It was quite simply the most beautiful tree that I had ever seen. It mirrored (on a much larger scale) an oak tree that stood in my garden back at home. Hang on, I thought to myself, 'my garden?' I started to think that actually I was simply a guardian and the tender of the land, rather than in any shape or perception, the owner. When I died, someone else would be looking after it…

This ancient looking oak tree displayed itself with strength, stability, and enduring beauty. It had deep roots which bizarrely I could see, that anchored itself firmly to the ground around it. There were seven major roots and all of them looked like they were massive hollow tubes – big enough to allow the passage of vast amounts of liquid or even possibly animals. Its branches were spread out wide and was providing shade and shelter for a variety of wildlife – I could not work out exactly what these animals were, but there were numerous scampering and flying beings.

The majesty of this ancient oak tree could be seen in its size and grandeur. It was very tall and had a massive, sturdy trunk that was enormous and thick with age. Its branches stretched out in all directions, creating a canopy that covered a large area. The leaves of this tree were typically green and glossy, but also with beautiful shades of gold, silver and red and yellow. I had never seen such beauty and strength in one thing ever! It simply filled me with awe. And it was wanting to speak to me!

I felt that this talking tree might be the embodiment of a particular aspect of nature, such as the spirit of the forest or the voice of the earth itself. It might even be offering its insights and knowledge to me, attuning to its energy and passing on ancient wisdom.

I started to perceive that the phrase 'follow the roots' was being ever repeated in my head, and that the two robed beings were nodding their heads at me in confirmation. There also followed a number of words and phrases that I did recognise but could not understand the logic or relevance. Words such as 'key', 'judgement', 'code', 'messenger'

I could sort of work out. Phrases included, 'source energy cells', and 'follow the markers' and 'destiny and hope are yours'. What a collection!

Then, as quickly as the vision had begun, it started to fade. The magnificent tree was first to go, melting into the cave wall, followed by the two elders who gently disappeared, smiling as they went. I actually think they were also waving as they went.

With reluctance, I took my hands from the cave wall and started to come back into my mind and body. Phew, that was some etherical journey. What had I learned? It seemed that my connection to ancient trees, in particular oaks, would give me insights into what it was I was meant to be doing, not only in my life, but in my surroundings too.

Ceres suddenly spoke, "come on we must be going, there is work to be done."

We continued on deeper into the cave, coming across a large chamber filled with crystal formations of all shapes and sizes. Some of the crystals were as small as pebbles, whilst others were as large as trees. The air in the chamber was filled with the faint hum of magic interspersed with the clicking sound of what sounded was a clock, and I could not help but feel a sense of wonder as I stood amongst the sparkling crystals.

Moving further, we came across a series of tunnels that led off in different directions from a central chamber. In the centre of the chamber was a large rock with a hole at its top. Ceres told me to climb onto his back and put my hand into the hole. I felt nervous to do so, as my irrational mind said there might be something in there, something that might bite. Of course, this trepidation was a childish thing, but it still seemed to be an issue to my confidence in physically doing it! Then a wave of certainty hit me – my Ceres would not get me to do something that would harm me, I was sure.

Now with a measure of confidence, I dipped my hand into the hole.

Ceres said, "grasp the first thing that your fingers touch and pull it out."

My fingertips got hold of something warm and rigid and I tightened around whatever it was and pulled it out. There in my hand was a beautiful oak wand – just as Ceres had predicted! It was around two foot long with three glowing red crystals in a line spaced evenly along the wand.

"This bright red one," said Ceres pointing to the one highest up the wand, "is red garnet, the fiery crystal of passion. It is considered one of the oldest crystals used for spiritual protection throughout the history on your planet. It will serve you well as a light in any dark space. It also represents the power to convert energies from one source to another and can break apart stagnant and dark energies. It will be useful for us where we are going."

"The middle one is red jasper", said Ceres. "It can ward off negative spirits and give you stability, security, and grounding. It is also a warrior's gem, so it brings an abundance of strength, courage and fearlessness. In a past life, you carried this as a centre gem in a breastplate of armour to show your enemies your power, but also your compassion. Again, it will serve us well."

"The final one of the three is red apatite, in your world quite rare to find. This beautiful crystal will enhance your focus, clarity, concentration, acceptance and unconditional love. This acceptance and unconditional love relates to you (the self) as well as from others. Apatite will expand your knowledge and truth as well as ease your sorrow, apathy, and anger. The priestesses of the Egyptian goddess Hathor wore apatite necklaces as well as carrying a staff adorned with apatite. A fitting trio of crystals to help us on our challenge ahead."

Ceres continued, "this wand is sacred to Jupiter and the wood of the oak is particularly sacred and powerful in its magic. We may need its power and energy, but at all times we must call in the energy of unconditional love if at all we feel a need to use it."

I was mesmerised by the wand – it felt as comfortable as an old set of gloves and built to take my hand as if the fingers were part of the wood itself. It was part of me.

"Ceres", I said, "what is that amulet you wear?"

A radiant amulet with a swirling core of golden and silver light, resembling a miniature galaxy hung from a chain around his neck.

"This is most scared, but I will tell you more later, as you will need to know how it helps me, and ultimately you."

Ceres and I moved towards a large glowing cavity to our front. It was if we were about to step off into somewhere else, or at least that's how my mind thought. Ceres simply said, "time to go."

CHAPTER 5

Tolerance

ROMAN ATTACK ON THE DRUIDS 77 AD

I became aware that Ceres and I were standing underneath a lake, which had a waterfall in front. When I say waterfall, perhaps a more accurate description would be 'water-rise' as the flow was going upwards. How mad was that? I touched the water-rise to confirm it was real water and not my complete imagination. By this stage my grasp with my inner conscious reality was fast running out. How can we be standing here underneath a lake? Perhaps this magnificent lake was a mirror?

To my immediate front there appeared to be nothing but hard ground, small scrubs and trees. Hmm, no mirror of a reflected lake then. I was staring upwards at the lake and could see ripples and small ringlets appearing like there were fish moving on its surface. It was all too bizarre.

We also had the large open space of the cave that we had exited behind us lit up with golden light and sparkling stones. These were new crystals the like of which I had never seen for their brilliance, colours and sizes.

In front Ceres stepped forward and seemed to be standing on a bridge although this was invisible, certainly to me anyway. Ceres beckoned me to move to him. I stepped forward, frightened and hesitant at first because I could not see where to put my foot down. But I did step out and whatever I'm stepping on feels sort of squashy. I looked down and there appeared to be pipes or tunnels running from the centre below us. I wonder if these were connected with the water above. They are see-through but nothing is inside them - for some reason I guess there are thoughts and energies flowing through – like a network of ideas – passages for information and thought.

Ceres then quietly said, "these tunnels are the roots of the tree you witnessed. Either one will take you to your past. Once you are there, you will learn a valuable lesson that you must take forward to your next life. You will be able to observe the 'you', but you cannot alter or change what is happening in front of you. To that end you will be 'invisible' most times – but there will be times that you are part of the scene and as such, can be heard and seen. Something will happen that will be part of a message or messages that you will take into the next life.

There you will impart that lesson to those around you for their good and for the good of humanity, as well of course, for your own growth."

"But" I stammered, "you are coming with me?"

"Of course, I will be there, but I will shift my shape into the wand you are holding. So, do not worry, I will be there with you. Now we must go, so chose a tunnel to enter."

I looked at the seven tunnel entrances and was drawn to the one closest to me and Ceres. A symbol adorned the entrance to the tunnel, and I realised I had seen something very similar in the cave earlier on in our journey high up on the cave walls.

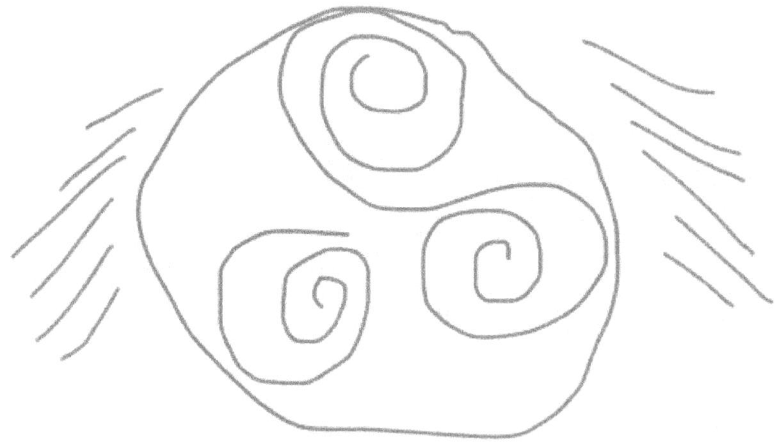

"Ah," said Ceres, "the druid symbol for everlasting life. Alternatively called the triskelion or the *triple spiral,* the triskele is a symbol closely associated with the sun, which is highly revered by the druids for being the source of all life. Some people believe the triskele symbol also represents life itself. Since all three spirals are drawn continuously and without any breaks, it is thought to symbolise the way life goes on and on, ever progressing, no matter what."

"Does that mean I am going back to Druid times?" I said.

"Who knows, and no one will know until you step into the tunnel. We do not know what we do not know. Come along, let's go," Ceres said somewhat impatiently.

So, this was it. I was about to go back in time and witness an event or events that had some crucial meaning to me and others. Having come so far in this journey, with a dragon of all things, I could hardly complain or object! Part of me felt apprehensive, part of me excited, and yet there was a tiny part of me that said 'don't go'!

"Are there any protocols that I should observe Ceres?" I said anxious to delay that moment of step off just a little bit.

"Protocols? Haha, good thinking but let's just go with it. You are this time, remember, an observer and there is nothing you can do or say that will change the past that you are visiting. No-one will see you, though it is possible they may *feel* your presence, but they will not smell you or be able to touch you. You are totally unseen, unheard and unknown."

In some ways that comforted me as whatever I would be witnessing, I could not impact on, or be asked to help with. I was to be utterly anonymous.

With that in mind, and grasping my wand tightly, I stepped into the tunnel. I was aware of a distant humming that seemed to be getting closer, my eyelids getting heavier and a general feeling of weightlessness. The tunnel was disintegrating from a solid shape into a green/yellow mist-like cloud. All of this was happening quickly, and a feeling of being dizzy in the head and starting to fall became a definite feeling that my body was undertaking some kind of change.

My eyelids started to lift, and I was aware of tumbling through the clouds and downwards towards green woods and fields. It was all coming up very quickly, and I naturally started to scream in anticipation of my hard collision with earth. Quite suddenly, everything went into slow motion and my descent slowed so dramatically that I thought I was looking down at a picture rather than planet earth!

I came to 'land' on a green field. When I say field, this was not a field with hedges and boundaries as I knew back home, but more overgrown and wilder pastureland with a plethora of beautiful wild grasses and flowers. In the distance I could see a large wood with what appeared to be massive oaks displaying their enormous green canopies, shading the ground below into a somewhat dark and forbidding place. That's where I was drawn to go.

As I walked towards the wood, my wand started to glow and vibrate in my hand.

"Welcome to Ancient Britain and the new rule of the Romans, Mike. The year is your 77 AD, and you will now meet the 'you', called Iseldir, an important Druid." Ceres spoke from the wand. "Let us see what happens, and what we shall learn…"

The Story of Iseldir and the plight of the Druids

Iseldir, Druid chieftain and temporary guardian of the Cup of Dreams walked alone to the ancient oak and yew tree thicket. This was a Sacred Centre with an ancient spring, trees that were centuries years old and a massive stone plinth to light a fire on. These three components are central to the druid cosmology belief, representing the Heavens, the Underworld, and the Mid-Earth, respectively.

He had always gone there when an important issue had to be resolved before he put it to the remainder of the druid grove or tribe. He preferred to do this on his own. For Iseldir, solitude was not a liability or strange. In solitude he could develop a deeper connection to his own inner voice and to the voices of the Kindred that lie within all of us. In solitude he became contemplative, centered, and discerning.

He also firmly believed that solitude was the staging ground for real, transformative change of thought and deeds. It was this transformation of thought that he strongly needed at this time judging from what he had heard amongst the tribes in the south.

There had been many whispers that the invasion force was destroying the culture they met in front of them. This was a disciplined force whose numbers of warriors and weaponry was by far superior to anything local people could offer as resistance. And the problem was they were getting closer to Iseldir and his people.

In the north part of what is now called Wales, his people had long been the centre of druidic culture and strength. The ancient ways passed down through generations had been lovingly preserved and nurtured. The Cup of Dreams was sign enough of the importance that Iseldir held among his folk and with the neighbouring tribes. These foreigners, called Romans, seemed to be determined to crush all those who opposed them, and to gain access to the local gold, silver and copper mines. Part of their strategy was also to take slaves in order to build their fortresses, towns and roads. From what Iseldir had gleaned, there was never any talk or peaceful negotiations, only confrontation, bloodshed and submission.

How was Iseldir going to protect his people and his neighbours? One thing they had as a real advantage over these Romans, was that they were on an island that could only be reached by crossing a strait of water that was both dangerous and unpredictable to those who did not know the currents.

As he sat in the Sacred Centre, he closed his eyes and called on his ancestors for advice. He had so many questions. What to do? How can he help understanding for both sides, both cultures? How can he communicate with the foreigners when he did not even know their language?

Then, an ancient spoke:

"Remember, we Druids are seen as a mysterious, ancient Celtic culture which has had a powerful presence in Britain and beyond for many centuries. Our culture is unique and highly respected, and our beliefs and practices are deeply rooted in our culture and religion.

When the Romans invaded Britain in 43 CE, we Druids initially were willing to tolerate the invaders, since we strongly believe in peaceful coexistence with other cultures. We believe in an honour code of respect and were willing to accept the Roman rule as long as we Druids were allowed to practice our own beliefs and customs. We were tolerant towards the invading Romans in many ways. We allowed them to establish their own religious practices, build temples, and even allowed some of their Roman gods to be worshipped.

Despite the Roman invasion, we chose to keep to our ancient beliefs and customs intact. We have also established trade relations with the Romans, which allowed them to continue to have access to goods and services. We also showed great tolerance in terms of law and justice. We allowed the Romans to set up their own legal system, and we respected Roman law. This was done in order to maintain peace and stability in the region. Despite the Romans' invasion, we also chose not to engage in armed conflict, and I urge you not to engage with them in a such a way.

We believe in peaceful coexistence and must not be interested in engaging in a war with them. We are thus very tolerant with the invading Romans, and we have showed a great deal of respect towards the Roman culture and beliefs. We do this in order to maintain peace and stability in the region and to ensure that our own beliefs and customs remained intact. Seek the revelations from the Cup of Dreams and go forward with compassion and tolerance in your heart."

Bizarrely as it had arrived, the ancient voice from ages past drifted off on the wind and into the trees and was gone.

Lying on his back and looking up at the massive oak tree canopy towering above him, Iseldir remembered the Cup of Dreams and the advice given to him by the previous holder, his father, Cymrolir. His advice was simple. Never drink from the Cup of Dreams unless the matter needing an answer was to protect the very existence of the Druids. Well, this appeared to be one of those times. Even better, the elders and all tribes were meeting for the ceremony of Beltane soon. There, as leader and chieftain, he could explain what he was going to do.

Iseldir took the Cup of Dreams from the bough of the most ancient tree in the grove, a mighty oak. It vibrated with an energy pulse that ran into all of his physical being. He paused for a short time, closed his eyes, and put his intention out – 'tell me how to communicate a message of tolerance to my people.'

The Cup itself, was not a cup as you or I would know. It was a simple carved piece of yew branch with a small hollow in its centre. It was covered in lichen such was its age. Reverently, Iseldir took it to the spring at the centre of the grove. Muttering a short phrase, "be and let it be" he dipped the branch into the spring water and held it there for a minute or two. He brought the Cup to his lips and drank the water from it, savouring the cold and crisp liquid.

A mist descended over him, but a brilliant light illuminated the mist, so it seemed like his was enshrouded with a golden cloak covering his whole being. With his eyes closed and muttering spells, Iseldir started to feel the message from the Cup of Dreams pulsing into his consciousness. What seemed like hours stood by the spring, actually only seconds, Iseldir opened his eyes knowing what he was to say to the elders and tribes come Beltane celebrations. Replacing the Cup of Dreams in its holding place back in the oak, he walked away from the grove and back to his village.

"Wow", I said to Ceres, "that was very intense. I wanted so much to speak with Iseldir and tell him how much I admired him."

"Haha, of course you admire him, that's because you are looking at yourself over 2,000 years ago! But however much you want to talk or shout out loud, he/you will never hear those words, never understand those feelings and emotions, for that is one of the sacred rules of travelling through time – leave no footprint, have no presence, observe only." Ceres responded. "I would say though, that I am sure you took in a valuable lesson from Iseldir. Important enough to take forward with you…"

"Well, as far as I could see, he was wrestling with this issue of the Romans and their conquest, and how to deal with them so that the Druid culture would not be threatened forever and at the very least would remain intact with a bit of give and take" I said. "The major lesson I take away from this is the ability to ask for help, and not try and do it all yourself. Iseldir has called on the ancestors to help him and looks like they have. We will have to see what Iseldir says to his people at Beltane."

Beltane was the celebration for the start of the summer season; Spring is fully realised, and new life is all around. This is also a time when the veils between worlds thin. We can look out to see fair folk progressing through the countryside, and the spirits of the trees, plants, animals, and places are singing with joy. The primal forces of spring have many guises - such as the Goddesses Danu, or Isolde, or the Gods Belanus, or Cerunnos, Lord of Wild things, but most of all, it is a time of hope and joy. This is exactly the energy I need to converse with the living, thought Iseldir!

The gathering was on top of a bare hill, so that hundreds of men, women and children could all attend and listen to the elders. It was an especially large congregation this Beltane due to the pressing issue of the Romans, and many tribes had travelled far to this point and listen to the Chieftain, Iseldir.

Ceres, occupying the shape of my wand, and myself climbed to the top of the hill alongside crowds of druid folk, young and old. The mood was one of laughter and high spirits among the young, and somewhat sober seriousness in the older folk. A semi-circle of five large stones marked the top of the hill and on them sat two elders either side of Iseldir who sat on the middle stone. Two large fires were already burning to one side, as the crowd sat/stood in a semi-circle in front of the elders.

Iseldir stood, staff in hand and beckoned the crowd for quiet. He raised his arms above his head to the sky and started the ceremony by calling in the quarters:

"I call upon the Spirit of the North, the Earth Mother, the Great Bear, to be with us in our sacred rite.
I call upon the Spirit of the East, the Skyfather, the Great Eagle, to be with us in our sacred rite.
I call upon the Spirit of the South, the Firebrother, the Great Dragon, to be with us in our sacred rite.

*I call upon the Spirit of the West, the Rainsister, the Great Whale,
to be with us in our sacred rite.*
And now, I call in the Spirits of place:
We call to the spirits of place, to those of Land, Sea and Sky, to
those of the three worlds to be with us in our sacred rite.

And now I call in our Ancestors:

We call to the ancestors of body, mind and spirit and water, the
great but forgotten communicator to be with us in our sacred rite. To
our ancestors whose tears and blood, joy and happiness have been felt
upon this land, whose songs course through our blood, and whose spirit
lives on through our celebrations, we call to you to be with us in our
sacred rite.

Here burn the twin fires of Beltane. Man and woman; God and
Goddess; Sky and Earth; each in each one of us. The Lady of the Land
takes the hand of the Green Lord, and between the two fires of God
and Goddess, of woman and man, is created the Bright One, the Child
of Light. Those who would, step forward now and pass through the
Beltane Gate. Pass through the fires and be renewed!"

Slowly the crowd moved through the gap between the two fires,
and all shouted 'Danu' in honour of the Goddess known for fertility
and wisdom. Once through, they all hurried back to their resting places
awaiting their Chieftains address.

And thus, Iseldir spoke:

"We Druids are respected and influential amongst the Celtic tribes,
and I have been approached to negotiate with the Romans. I will act as
an interpreter and intermediary between the two sides, conveying messages
between the Celts and Romans. We have also served as advisors to the
Celts, helping them to make informed decisions about their interactions
with the invaders. We can use the knowledge of the Roman culture, the

environment, and the political situation to advise our Celtic brothers and sisters regarding the Romans. We all know that the Romans will impose their own culture and laws on the Celts, and that the best way to preserve the Celtic culture is to reach a compromise with the invaders. By doing this we will also protect our culture and way of life.

I had the ancients speak to me through the Cup of Dreams. They confirmed that we must not use force or intimidation. Instead, we use the careful language of understanding and tolerance. Tolerance does not mean agreement or approval of others beliefs and behaviours, but rather an acceptance that others have the right to hold and express their own beliefs and practices. It is important to practice tolerance in order to create a more inclusive and harmonious society.

Can we trust the Romans I hear you say? That is always the difficulty facing the inhabitants of an invaded country. But my feelings, brothers and sisters, is that if we go to them, with open arms, no talk of violence, no threats, simply with options for them, then with our tolerance towards the foreigners, maybe they will leave us alone to follow our path.

So, unless anyone says otherwise, I will go to these invaders and tell them that we offer nothing but advice and help. I will say to them that sharing some of our precious resources and skills is not a problem provided we can do what we have done for eons. We want to show them that we are a tolerant people and not savages. That's all I have to say on the matter."

Some cheering started up, but in the main, all Iseldir could hear was muttering and, looking at the faces around him, he could see their concern and even a rebellious twinkle in the eyes.

"Come Mike", said Ceres, "we need to move on."

"But should we not stay with Iseldir and see his meeting with the Romans and its aftermath?"

"No, not unless you want to see butchery and the wiping out of all those souls you saw tonight! The truth is, Iseldir sold the idea of a tolerant life with the Romans, but that only lasted about a year. With the arrival of a new Roman General Gnaeus Julius Agricola came a determination of complete druid genocide. Some escaped and kept their movement alive for thousands of years in secret, but largely they and their ancient ways were forgotten. We must go now."

Ceres turned and started to walk through the forest.

"But Ceres, what is the true lesson here for me?"

Ceres sighed and said, "One of the obvious lessons is that people change – one the one hand Iseldir made an honourable pact with the invading forces in an attempt to save his people from what had happened elsewhere on this land. On the other hand, nothing is always the same as we progress through time – different personalities bring about differing views, and so change is inevitable."

Mike followed Ceres reluctantly, his mind swirling with the weight of what he had just witnessed and the grim truth Ceres had revealed. The Druids' attempt at peace, noble as it was, had ultimately failed in the face of shifting Roman ambitions.

Yet, Mike couldn't help but feel there was more to learn from Iseldir's story than just the inevitability of change.

As they walked through the misty forest, Ceres spoke again, her voice calm but firm. "Mike, there are deeper lessons here for you. Let me guide you through them."

"Iseldir's approach was rooted in tolerance and understanding," Ceres began. "He sought to bridge the gap between his people and the Romans by offering peace and cooperation. This is a powerful lesson in itself - true leadership often requires humility and a willingness to compromise. But tolerance alone is not enough when faced with those who see kindness as weakness."

Mike nodded, understanding the nuance. "So, it's about balance? Being tolerant but not naive?"

"Exactly," Ceres replied. "You must temper your openness with discernment. Recognise when others are acting in good faith and when their intentions may be more self-serving. Iseldir's mistake was not in his tolerance but in underestimating how quickly circumstances - and people - can change."

Ceres continued, "Another lesson lies in the fleeting nature of alliances. Iseldir's agreement with the Romans was built on mutual benefit, but such arrangements are only as strong as the individuals upholding them. When Agricola arrived, he had no loyalty to Iseldir's vision of peace."

Mike frowned. "So, does that mean we shouldn't trust anyone?"

"No," Ceres said gently. "It means you must build relationships on a foundation that can withstand change. Trust is important, but so is preparing for contingencies when trust is broken. Be adaptable, Mike. Learn to pivot when circumstances demand it."

Ceres paused and gestured to a clearing where ancient oak trees stood tall and proud, their branches intertwined like an eternal embrace. "Though the Druids were nearly wiped out, their legacy endured in secret for centuries. Their reverence for nature, their wisdom - it all persisted because a few brave souls refused to let it die."

Mike looked at the trees and felt their quiet strength. "So even when everything seems lost, there's always hope if someone carries the torch?"

"Yes," Ceres said with a smile. "Your actions today may not bear fruit in your lifetime, but they can plant seeds for future generations.

Never underestimate the power of resilience and the importance of preserving what truly matters."

Finally, Ceres turned to Mike with a piercing gaze. "Iseldir knew his people were afraid. He knew many disagreed with him, yet he stood firm in his convictions and acted for what he believed was their best chance at survival. Leadership is not about pleasing everyone - it's about making difficult choices and accepting responsibility for their consequences."

Mike took a deep breath as he processed his words.

"So, being a leader means having courage even when others doubt you?"

"Yes," Ceres affirmed. "But remember, courage must be paired with wisdom and foresight. Iseldir's intentions were noble, but he lacked a plan for what might happen if the Romans betrayed him. True leadership requires both heart and strategy."

By the time they emerged from the forest into a new scene from history, Mike felt a renewed sense of purpose. The story of Iseldir and his people wasn't just a tale of tragedy; it was a testament to resilience, adaptability, and the enduring power of human spirit - even in the face of overwhelming odds.

"Thank you, Ceres," Mike said quietly.

Ceres smiled knowingly. "The journey isn't over yet. Let us see where to next. But before we depart to whichever time zone you choose next, I promised to tell you a little more about the time I grew up and attended school – well this was actually called the Dragon's Academy…"

"Oh yes please Ceres," said Mike, "tell me all about it!"

CHAPTER SIX

Life in the Dragon's Academy

Dragons Academy

"My younger years were a time of immense learning and preparation, a period that shaped me into this majestic and wise dragon that you see in front of you today – haha."

Born of cosmic origins, I was sent to the Dragons Academy, a revered institution where young dragons were trained, not only in their natural abilities, but also in the profound responsibilities of their existence. My time at the academy was both challenging and transformative, and I mastered skills that would later define my role as a guardian and guide across dimensions and time.

The Dragons Academy is truly a breathtaking and otherworldly institution, nestled in a unique cosmos called *Luminara Sanctum*, located an astounding three billion light-years from the mysterious *Sea of Nu* where I was born.

This cosmos is vibrant with swirling nebulae and shimmering stars that seem close enough to touch. A radiant name suggesting light, hope, and guidance in the vast cosmos. The surrounding environment is alive with energy flows that dragons tap into during their training. The air itself hums with power, invigorating every being within its reach.

This academy is not merely a school but a realm of wonder, designed to foster the growth and mastery of young dragons destined for cosmic responsibilities. So, not all dragons were permitted entrance into the Academy, I was truly luck to be accepted.

So, what does the Academy look like? It is primarily built within vast, interconnected caves. These caves are illuminated by radiant crystals embedded in the walls, which emit a soft, ethereal glow. These crystals not only provide light but also pulse with energy, resonating with the life force of the dragons within.

Scattered throughout the academy are massive doors that, when opened, reveal enormous amphitheatres. These spaces serve as classrooms where dragons gather to learn advanced skills such as shape-shifting, invisibility, celestial manipulation, and a whole host of other skills. The amphitheatres are designed to accommodate dragons of all sizes, with towering ceilings and acoustics that amplify even the softest voice.

There are also the training chambers which are specialised chambers dedicated to honing specific abilities. For example:

Shape-shifting rooms **contain mirrors and magical artifacts to aid in mastering transformations.** *Pulse burst transmission halls* **are equipped with energy conduits that help young dragons practice sending precise energy signals across vast distances.** *Invisibility arenas* **simulate diverse environments to teach dragons how to manipulate light and energy seamlessly.**

Some parts of the academy open up into celestial domes where the younger dragons can observe and interact with cosmic phenomena. These domes are used for training in controlling super moons and super tides, offering a direct connection to the forces they will one day guide.

Halls of Balance. A sacred area within the academy is dedicated to instilling the principles of harmony and stewardship. These halls are adorned with murals depicting dragons aiding various dimensions, serving as a reminder of their profound responsibilities.

One of the first lessons I learned was *shape-shifting*. This ability allows dragons to adapt to their surroundings, assuming forms that would enable them to blend seamlessly into different worlds. For me, this meant that I could walk among humans without causing fear or chaos, appearing as one of them when necessary. Shape-shifting required not just physical transformation but also an understanding of the essence of the form being assumed. I practiced tirelessly, learning to mimic human movements, expressions, and even emotions so convincingly that I could pass unnoticed in any society.

I did once have a problem trying to assume the shape of a mathematical ruler. I wanted to get into a school classroom so that by being a ruler, I would be picked up and used by children. From that physical contact I would be able to 'read' a normal child's mind, so that if I ever had to assume the shape of a child, I would have the necessary reactions and emotions. However, I could never fully understand the principle of being flat, and this meant I had to forgo that shape and concentrate on being a pencil instead! Over time though, I did manage to acquire the skill of being flat – no easy task I can tell you!

Another critical skill taught at the academy was *power communication*, a unique ability that allows us dragons to summon aid from others of our kind through a technique called pulse burst transmission. This involves sending out powerful waves of energy pulses that carry messages across vast distances. This technique requires immense focus and control, as each pulse had to be perfectly calibrated to convey urgency without causing disruption. I excelled in this art, earning recognition for my ability to transmit signals with clarity and precision.

The academy also trained young dragons in the art of *invisibility*. This wasn't merely about vanishing from sight; it was about mastering the ability to manipulate light and energy around oneself. Invisibility requires a deep understanding of one's environment and a connection to the natural flows of energy within it. I found this particularly fascinating, as it allowed me to observe without interference, gaining insights into the lives of those I would later guide – like you for example!

One of the most advanced teachings at the academy involves controlling *super moons* and *super tides*. These celestial phenomena had profound effects on the Earth's ecosystems, influencing animal migrations, ocean currents, and even human behaviour. Dragons like me were taught how to harness these forces to aid both animals and humans in times of need. For instance, by subtly shifting the gravitational pull during a super moon, I could help guide stranded marine animals back to safety or ensure that crops received much-needed irrigation during critical periods.

Perhaps most importantly, I learned about my role as a guardian of balance. The academy instilled in its students a deep sense of responsibility toward all living beings. Dragons are not merely powerful creatures; they are stewards of harmony, tasked with using our abilities to protect and nurture life across dimensions. I took these lesson to heart, understanding that my powers were not for domination but for service.

Of course, one of the things everyone expects a dragon to do is to fly and breathe fire. The flying bit was easy enough but the fire breathing took a little more to get expert at it. I will tell you more about that at another time.

Through years of rigorous training and countless trials, I grew into a dragon of extraordinary capability and wisdom. Yet it wasn't just my mastery of skills that defined me - it was my compassion and unwavering commitment to fostering understanding between beings. Even as a young dragon, I demonstrated an innate ability to connect with others on a profound level, laying the foundation for my future role as a guide through time.

The lessons from my youth at the Dragon Academy have stayed with me throughout my life. These were not merely tools but principles that shape my every action. Whether summoning help through power communication or using super tides to assist those in need, my abilities were always guided by a deep sense of purpose: to bridge divides, nurture life, and uphold truth across all realms.

Anyway, young man, enough of the history lesson as this all happened many eons ago. It is time once again to travel, and you need to choose a tunnel.

"Yes of course Ceres", said Mike. "I can see there are only six left in front of me."

"That is because once you entered the realm of the Druids and Romans, that portal has closed – forever. You need to choose a new tunnel."

CHAPTER SEVEN

Love

NEW WORLD DISCOVERY THE NORSEMAN 790 AD

Mike chose a tunnel with deliberate care, his fingers tracing the ancient markings that seemed to pulse beneath his touch. The air inside carried the weight of millennia, thick with an energy that made the fine hairs on his neck rise. Beside him, Ceres moved with fluid grace, his massive form somehow both intimidating and reassuring in the confined space.

The dragon's amulet caught Mike's attention - not merely glowing, but containing what appeared to be a living cosmos, stars being born and dying in its crystalline depths. Its light cast strange shadows that made the tunnel markings appear to dance and shift, telling stories in a language lost to time.

"Mike." Ceres' voice resonated directly in his mind, a symphony of ancient power and gentle guidance.

"The vortex manifests from the collective wisdom of those who walked these paths before. It will guide you, but you must learn to trust what lies beyond sight."

A portal materialised like the northern lights condensed into a doorway, its edges crackling with possibilities. Mike *felt* rather than *heard* the whispers of countless generations, their knowledge condensed into fragments of thought: "Balance... harmony... courage...love…" Each word carried weight, as if spoken by the earth itself.

A tremor shook the tunnel and brought with it a presence that felt wrong - a corruption of the ancient magic that permeated these halls. A shadowy creature emerged baring eyes like dying stars, its form a mockery of natural law. Yet when Ceres moved to defend Mike, his power manifested not as raw force but as a barrier of pure harmony of golden light, its beauty singing in counterpoint to the creature's discord. Whatever it was, simply disappeared.

As Mike ran deeper into the tunnel, the symbols on the walls began to tell a story: of Vikings crossing vast oceans, of first contacts between peoples, of a dragon who walked through time itself. The ancient markings shifted and flowed, showing him glimpses of what was to come.

The scene then shifted to 790 AD, where northern lights painted the sky in sheets of ethereal color. The longship Havmann cut through frigid waters, its dragon-headed prow splitting waves that could swallow lesser vessels whole. The journey had already claimed two ships from their original fleet of five - one lost to a storm off the Faroe Islands, another crushed by ice near Greenland's treacherous coast.

Erik the Wise stood at his ship's prow, his weather-worn face marked not just by age but by the wisdom earned through countless voyages. His eyes, the colour of storm-tossed seas, scanned the horizon where strange birds wheeled and called.

They had followed these birds for three days, knowing they must signal land ahead. The salt-laden wind carried unfamiliar scents - pine forests, fresh water, and something else, something new.

Beside him, Freydis the Bold wore her battle-scars like jewellery, each one a testament to victories won through cunning rather than mere strength. She had been the one to insist they press on when the crew's spirits flagged, her voice rising above the howling wind to remind them of the glory that awaited in undiscovered lands. Her fingers traced the runestone hanging at her throat - a gift from her grandmother, who had dreamed of western shores but never lived to see them.

The remaining crew, forty strong, had been transformed by the journey. Gone were the boisterous raiders who had set out from Norway's fjords. In their place stood lean, quiet warriors who had learned to read the moods of sky and sea, who had watched their companions succumb to the ocean's fury and emerged with a deeper respect for nature's power. They had followed ancient navigation techniques - the position of the sun, the patterns of stars, the behaviour of waves - while adding their own discoveries to this accumulated wisdom.

Mike was looking down on this scene like a helicopter hovering overhead. It was at that point that something suddenly gave way and Mike fell into the churning waters, the moment crystallised into something more than mere accident.

Ceres' sudden intervention became a bridge between worlds - his magic not just a display of power, but a demonstration of the harmony possible between peoples divided by time, culture and the air itself!

The shock of impact drove the air from Mikes' lungs. The weight of his clothes dragged him down as the fierce current caught him, pulling him away from the ship. Through the murky water, he saw indigenous canoes approaching the longship, their occupants' expressions shifting from diplomatic caution to alarm at his sudden appearance. Above, Ceres dove towards the water, his massive form casting a shadow across the waves.

Mike fought against the crushing cold, his limbs already growing numb. The intersection of two worlds – Viking and indigenous – swirled around his brain as chaotically as the waters themselves. In that moment, suspended between sky and sea, past and present, he understood why Ceres had brought him here. Some moments in history hinged not on grand gestures but on small accidents, on how people chose to react when the unexpected disrupted their carefully laid plans.

Ceres's dive was silent but powerful, his wings folded close as he streaked toward the water like golden lightning. The dragon's amulet flared brilliantly, and suddenly the churning waters around Mike grew still, forming a perfect cylinder of calm in the midst of chaos. Mike felt himself being lifted by an unseen force, water streaming from his clothes as he rose through the air in a cocoon of dragon-magic.

The indigenous warriors and Norse crew alike stood transfixed as Ceres curved gracefully upward, his massive form banking against the aurora-lit sky. The dragon's scales reflected the northern lights, creating a display that merged natural wonder with supernatural power. With careful precision, he deposited Mike onto the Havmann's deck, where Freydis immediately wrapped him in a heavy fur cloak.

The magic that had saved Mike lingered in the air, a tangible reminder that they were witnessing something beyond ordinary human experience. Ceres landed with impossible delicacy on the longship's prow, his weight somehow not disturbing the vessel's balance. The dragon's presence transformed what could have been a moment of tragedy into one of wonder, his intervention bridging the gap between the two peoples who watched in awe.

Askook, the indigenous leader in the lead canoe, proved to be more than just a witness to this incredible event. His eyes held an ancient knowledge that recognised Ceres not as a creature of myth, but as a guardian of balance. When he shared stories around the fire that night, his words painted pictures of spirits that walked between worlds, of guardians who maintained the delicate balance between nature and human ambition.

Ceres had spread a talking net over the two groups so that they could understand each other for this first moment of contact between an indigenous nation and sea farers from across the 'great water'.

The music that rose from both groups transcended mere cultural exchange. The indigenous elder's song spoke of cycles of time and the interconnectedness of all things, while Freydis' Norse ballad carried echoes of the same eternal truths, dressed in different metaphors. As their voices twined together beneath the aurora's dance, even Ceres added his own harmonic resonance - a deep thrumming that seemed to connect earth and sky.

Erik stood up the fire light illuminating his face. "who are you, how have you come to this place and where are you going?" he asked Mike directly.

Erik's question to Mike about the future hung in the air like the smoke from their fire, carrying the weight of possibilities yet to unfold. In that moment, surrounded by the blending of cultures and watched over by a being who transcended time itself, Mike understood that he wasn't just witnessing history - he was part of its living tapestry, where past and future wove together in patterns too complex for any single perspective to fully grasp.

"I cannot explain fully, only that for you and for Askook's people I am here to listen, to offer help if that is needed, but mostly to enjoy your company."

The firelight painted shadows on faces that had begun the day as strangers and would end it as something more - not quite friends, perhaps, but fellow travellers on a journey that stretched far beyond the physical realm. In their shared songs and stories, they had found something universal: the eternal human quest for understanding, for connection, for love that transcends the boundaries of time and culture.

As the night deepened and stars wheeled overhead, Mike felt the weight of his role in this cosmic dance. He was no longer just an observer but a participant in a story that had been unfolding since the first humans looked up at the stars and dared to dream of what lay beyond their known world.

The exchange around the fire grew deeper as the night progressed. Askook's people brought forth sacred objects - a ceremonial pipe carved with symbols that eerily matched some Mike had seen in the tunnel, and a drum whose rhythms seemed to make the very air vibrate with meaning. The Norse crew shared their own treasures: amber beads that caught the firelight like trapped souls, and a drinking horn etched with tales of the World Tree.

Leif the Curious had begun to grasp fragments of the indigenous language when they spoke to each other rather than directly at the Norsemen, his quick mind building bridges between words. "Manitou," he repeated carefully, understanding dawning in his eyes as Askook explained through gestures the concept of spiritual power that resided in all things. It wasn't so different from the Norse belief in fylgjur—the spirit that accompanied each person through life.

Ceres watched this exchange with ancient eyes that held memories of countless such meetings. Through their mental link, Mike caught glimpses of other times, other shores - Phoenicians meeting the people of Britannia, Greek traders encountering Egyptian priests, Polynesians finding new islands across vast seas. Always there had been this delicate moment of choice between conflict and connection.

The dragon's presence affected each person differently. To the Norse, he embodied their tales of mighty wyrms and cosmic serpents. To the indigenous people, he represented the thunderbirds of their legends - beings of power who maintained the balance of the world. Both interpretations were true in their way, yet neither captured the full complexity of what Ceres truly was.

An elderly woman from Askook's tribe approached Mike with slow, deliberate steps. Her face was a map of wrinkles, each line earned through years of wisdom. She carried a small pouch made of deerskin, and from it withdrew a handful of what looked like ordinary pebbles.

But as she arranged them in a pattern on the ground, Mike saw they were fragments of crystals that caught the firelight in ways that seemed impossible, creating miniature echoes of the aurora overhead.

Through Leif's growing vocabulary and elaborate hand gestures, she conveyed a story: long ago, her people had encountered beings who walked between worlds, guardians who left behind tokens of their passage. The crystals were said to be tears of these beings, shed when they witnessed both the great beauty and terrible cruelty humans were capable of.

As she spoke, Ceres lowered his massive head until one of his eyes was level with the crystal arrangement. A resonance built between dragon and stones, causing them to emit a soft, pulsing light that matched the rhythm of the amulet around his neck. The old woman nodded as if confirming something she had long suspected.

Erik watched this display with keen interest, his merchant's mind already grasping the implications of this connection between his people's legends and those of this new land. But Freydis saw something deeper - a pattern that suggested all their journeys, all their stories, were part of something larger, a tapestry being woven across time itself.

Mike observed how love manifested in unexpected ways throughout the gathering. It showed in the gentle way Askook helped an elder adjust her fur wrap against the cooling night air, in the protective stance of Norse warriors who had once been strangers but now guarded both groups equally, in the shared laughter that needed no translation.

Through his mental link with Ceres, Mike felt the dragon's ancient wisdom unfold: love was not just an emotion but a force as fundamental as gravity, binding together not just people but the very fabric of existence. He saw how it had guided the Norse across treacherous seas, not just for glory or wealth, but for the deep human need to connect, to understand, to grow. He witnessed it in the indigenous people's willingness to share their fire despite their initial fear, in their courage to reach across the divide of language and custom.

A young Norse child, who had somehow maintained her innocence through the harsh journey, approached an indigenous girl clutching a decorated clay doll. Without hesitation, the Norse child offered her most prized possession - a carved wooden horse, worn smooth from countless hours of play. The indigenous girl reciprocated by sharing her doll. Their interaction, pure and untainted by adult prejudices, demonstrated what Ceres had been trying to teach Mike all along.

"Love," Ceres spoke in Mike's mind, "is the force that allows humans to transcend their greatest limitations. It is what gives them the courage to cross oceans, the wisdom to choose peace over conflict, the strength to trust in the face of uncertainty. This is the lesson hidden in every tunnel marking, encrypted in every ancient story."

Mike understood then that his journey through the tunnels, his witnessing of this historic encounter, was about more than observing the past. It was about understanding how love - in all its forms - had been the constant force driving human progress, innovation, and connection. Whether expressed through Freydis's fierce protection of her crew, Erik's diplomatic wisdom, or Askook's generous sharing of his people's sacred knowledge, love was the underlying current that made meaningful connection possible.

The crystals the elder had laid out caught the last flickers of firelight, their pattern now clearly forming the same symbol Mike had seen repeated in the tunnel markings - a simple yet profound representation of interconnectedness, of the eternal dance between different peoples, different times, different worlds. All bound together by the most fundamental force in the universe: love's endless capacity to bridge the unbridgeable.

Slowly, as the dawn lit up the horizon, Mike walked quietly away from the fireside and walked over to Ceres sitting a distance away.

"What an amazing connection we have witnessed, and a promise that the future holds between people's coming together without fear and treachery".

"Oh that it were so," Ceres replied, "it is not always so clear cut. But now that you have seen the emotion 'love', we must move on."

Discovering Solarys

Mike: "Ceres, this amulet you wear - it's mesmerising. That swirling light at its core, it feels... alive. What is it? And how did it come to be yours?"

Ceres: "Ah, Mike, so you've noticed Solarys again. I did promise you earlier to speak about this, and before we journey again, this is something I must impart to you. It is no ordinary amulet, but an ancient entity of profound wisdom and power. Its history is intertwined with my own, and its purpose extends far beyond me, actually to guide us both on our journeys."

Mike: "Guide us? You mean it's more than just a symbol?"

Ceres: "Much more. Solarys was bestowed upon me during my time at the Dragon Academy, to understand the cosmic forces that bind all realms together. The Celestial Council of Dragons created Solarys as a reward for my efforts and as a tool to help me fulfil my destiny."

"Ok you have already told me about the Dragon Academy? That all sounds incredible. What did you do to earn something so extraordinary?" said Mike.

Ceres smiled and answered. "It was not a single act but rather a culmination of my studies, my perseverance, and my willingness to embrace the interconnectedness of all things. Solarys was given to me because I demonstrated the potential to guide others - not just dragons, but beings across all realms. The Council saw in me the capacity to bridge divides and protect those who seek enlightenment."

Mike looked inquisitively. "So, what exactly does Solarys do? I mean, besides looking like a miniature galaxy hanging from your neck."

"Solarys is far more than it appears," said Ceres. "It is a repository of ancient knowledge - a living archive of forgotten histories, celestial alignments, and magical lore. It senses disruptions in the flow of time or energy and warns us of impending challenges. Its wisdom transcends the physical and temporal planes, offering guidance not only to me but also to you when the moment calls for it."

"Wait - me? How does it help me?" said Mike.

"Through subtle nudges - visions, dreams, or moments of clarity when you need them most. You may not always realise its influence, but Solarys has already been guiding you toward understanding your purpose." Ceres grinned as he replied.

"That's... humbling. But why would something so powerful care about me?"

"Because your path is tied to mine, Mike. Together, we are part of something much larger - a cosmic tapestry that weaves together realms and destinies. Solarys exists to ensure we stay true to our paths while protecting us when needed."

Solarys (speaking for the first time): "Indeed, Mike. You are as integral to this journey as Ceres himself. My purpose is not solely to guide him but to illuminate truths for both of you. The challenges ahead will test your resolve and your unity."

Mike (startled): "It speaks! Wait - you speak! Solarys... what do you mean by challenges ahead?"

Solarys: "The balance of realms is delicate, and forces seek to disrupt it. Together with Ceres, you will face trials that require courage, wisdom, and compassion. My role is to prepare you both - to amplify Ceres' abilities when needed and shield you from harm in dire moments."

Mike: "Amplify abilities? Like what?"

Ceres: "Solarys enhances my connection to cosmic energies - strengthening my magic, sharpening my foresight, and even shielding us from malevolent forces. It acts as a bridge between dimensions, enabling communication with ethereal beings who hold crucial knowledge for our quest."

Mike: "So it's like having an ancient mentor watching over us?"

Ceres (chuckling): "A poetic way of putting it - but yes. Solarys is both guide and protector. It reminds me of my responsibilities as your mentor while ensuring I don't lose sight of my own growth."

Solarys: "And remember this, Mike - your bond with Ceres is no accident. Just as he guides you through history and transformation, so too do you remind him of the importance of humanity's resilience and potential for growth."

Mike (quietly): "I never thought I'd be part of something so... vast."

Ceres: "None of us truly expect it until we are called upon. But take heart - you are not alone in this journey. With Solarys' wisdom and our shared strength, we will face whatever lies ahead together."

Solarys (gently): "Indeed. The light within me mirrors the light within each of you - a reminder that even amidst darkness, there is always a path forward if we have the courage to seek it."

CHAPTER NINE

Empathy

ALFRED THE GREAT 878 AD

I turned and looked around me. The landscape was changing in front
of my face, like an artist washing in a new background colour. The
fields and woods blurred into a dark grey patina which started to take
on the form of cliffs and hills. We were back facing the tunnels, but
now there were six, the seventh one magically closing as I watched and
becoming solid stone.

A shadow poured over me like a wave. Ceres was back in all his
'dragonus' beauty – no longer a wand as before but as a magnificent
creature, multiple colours and textures whom I had the privilege to
journey with.

"Go with your heart", Ceres said, nodding at the openings.

With that I walked into the first tunnel entrance I could and saw it
grow in front of me as Ceres put the first of his enormous feet/claw at
the entrance.

Another strange 'etching' adorned the entrance to the opening, and
again, I remembered it from the strange carvings I had seen previously
high up in the cave wall.

"Ah", said Ceres, " this I believe means we are travelling to your
so called 'Dark Ages', a leap of half a millennia from Iseldir's time.
Where in the world are we going though I wonder?"

And thus, the opening grew to a tremendous size allowing the ease of passage for Ceres to walk alongside me.

The subliminal colours of the tunnel glowed with an almost plasma type energy, constantly moving in an etherical veil like a curtain being drawn which reminded me of the Northern Lights. Oranges mixed with purples along with aqua blue and pink bathed us in extraordinary light as we moved along the passage. It was quite beautiful as well as being rather mysterious.

It suddenly became darker and we left the lights behind us as we pushed on. It got so dark that I started to trip over my own feet and had to reach out and hold onto Ceres to stop me from falling.

"Use your wand, whispered Ceres, as I can see perfectly but obviously, you cannot!"

I had forgotten about the wand which was strapped to my belt. I pulled it out and almost without pause the red garnet started to emit light. I remembered Ceres telling me previously that it would serve me well as a light in any dark space. And sure enough, it did! Once I could see properly, I was amazed at the height of the tunnel. I sort of imagined it to be, perhaps ten feet to the celling, but it was actually at least ten times that, so high that even my beautiful red light could not even illuminate the top. Glowing mosses and lichen ran all the way up, which showed there must be a source of water from above nourishing the plant life on the walls.

We continued along the now twisting tunnel and before long, I could see it getting lighter with a pinprick of white light showing itself. As we walked the pinprick became bigger and bigger, until at last we came to 'the other side'. Here we go again I thought, as I stepped out from the tunnel and into the open.

Actually, it was not the open countryside but a dwelling of some kind. The walls were made up of lengths of timber, some thick, some just long sticks with mud seemingly holding everything together. It appeared to be in a rectangular shape and of a reasonable size. There was a hole in the roof and a smoldering fire in the centre. Along with some blackened pots and what appeared to be a reed/rushes bed space, that was all to the dwelling. No windows, no people, very simple indeed. I could hear noises outside, what sounded like horses and people, and I peered through a hole in the door.

Outside was a muddy track with people dressed in what appeared to be medieval clothing, rough and dirty cassock style robes with leather boots, pulling horse drawn carts brimming with straw and wood. Similar buildings straddled the track and it very much seemed that we were in a large village or small town.

"Should I go outside?" I said to Ceres.

"Of course, you must, that's why we are here! Don't worry about what you look like, as both you and I are invisible to them this time. They cannot see or hear us," replied Ceres. "My advice would be to follow the people and see what is happening. My feeling is we are in an Anglo Saxon town, although I am not picking up where we are other than it's what you would call England."

Gingerly I pushed open the door and stepped out into, who knows where…?

The first thing I noticed was that it was definitely warm, much warmer outside than it was in the hut I had just left. It must be Spring or Summer I thought. Everyone seemed to be going the same way, and that was downhill.

From what I could see at first glance, the village was situated in a rural area, surrounded by fields and forests with quite a substantial river running through the middle. The landscape was dotted with small cottages made of wood and straw, with thatched roofs and wattle and daub walls. It was also surrounded by a low stone wall probably for protection against raiders and wild animals, although in places there were men building it even higher.

The villagers seemed to be mostly farmers and craftsmen. The men were wearing simple tunics and trousers, while the women wore long dresses and headscarves. There were plenty of children running around playing games, chasing after chickens and goats, and generally getting under everyone's feet!

We approached what appeared to be the centre of the village, which was a large open space, presumably where the villagers gathered for important events and celebrations. There was also a small church, quite plain but held in reverence by the villagers. There was also a much larger and grander building, if you could call any of the buildings grand, which I assumed must belong to the tribal leader or chieftain.

It was here that the village had their marketplace, this was where traders came to sell their wares and buy local produce. The market was a bustling hub of activity, with people haggling over prices, and artisans showcasing their skills. There were blacksmiths, carpenters, potters, and weavers, all displaying their wares and offering their services. I would say in all there must have been about a hundred people milling around, going about their daily business.

As the sun sets, the villagers retire to their homes, lighting candles and oil lamps to ward off the darkness. The sounds of animals settling in for the night mingle with the laughter and chatter of the villagers as they gather around the fire to share stories and songs. The village is quiet, but alive with the promise of a new day to come.

As I moved to the edge of the gathering of people, I listened to what they had to say. From what I could gather, we were in a Saxon village called Wintanceaster in the Kingdom of Wessex and their ruler and hero was the son of Ethelwulf, called Alfred. It was fully apparent that these people regarded Alfred as a very successful warrior king protecting them against the Danes and Vikings.

They were also laughing about his hideout in the swamps and marshes to avoid capture some years before, and how he emerged victorious to lead his people once again in their struggle to keep peace in and on the land.

As I looked around at the men sitting beside the fire (there were no women), I saw an American tribal chief in full feather headgear. I rubbed my eyes as this was totally weird! How can that be – I thought? Then I realised that he was looking directly at me and smiling! He could see me! As the mysterious Native American chief locked eyes with me, I felt a surge of confusion and curiosity. How could he see me when Ceres had assured me that we were invisible to the villagers? The chief's smile was warm and knowing, as if he held secrets that I had yet to uncover.

Intrigued, I approached him cautiously, wondering if he would speak or if this was simply a figment of my imagination. To my surprise, he nodded and gestured for me to sit beside him near the crackling fire. As I settled down, the chief began to speak in a language I couldn't understand, yet somehow, the meaning of his words became clear in my mind.

"You are a traveller from a distant time and place," he said, his voice resonating with wisdom. "Your journey has brought you here to witness a crucial moment in history, one that will shape the future of this land and its people."

I leaned in closer, eager to learn more about the purpose of my visit to this Saxon village. The chief continued, "The great King Alfred, whom the villagers speak of with such reverence, faces a critical decision that will determine the fate of his kingdom. He must choose between his own pride and the well-being of his people."

The chief's words hung heavy in the air as I pondered their significance. I turned to Ceres, who had been silently observing our exchange, and asked, "What decision must King Alfred make? And how can we help guide him towards the right path?"

Ceres replied, "King Alfred must decide whether to engage in a dangerous battle against the invading Danes or to seek a peaceful resolution through diplomacy. The outcome of this decision will have far-reaching consequences for the future of your kingdom of England and the world as we know it."

As I absorbed this information, the chief spoke once more, "You have been chosen to bear witness to this pivotal moment and to offer your wisdom to the great king. Trust in your instincts and the knowledge you have gained from your travels through time."

With a final nod, the chief disappeared as mysteriously as he had appeared, leaving me with a sense of purpose and determination. I turned to Ceres and said, "We must find a way to speak with King Alfred and guide him towards the path of peace. The future depends on it."

Together, Ceres and I set off into the village, ready to embark on our meeting with the King – where would this take us, and how will we be received I wondered?

As Ceres and I made our way through the village, I couldn't help but feel a deep sense of empathy for the people around us.

Though we were invisible to them, I could see the struggles and hardships etched on their faces. The weight of the impending decision by King Alfred seemed to hang heavy in the air, affecting every man, woman, and child in Wintanceaster.

We approached the grand building where we believed King Alfred resided, and as we drew closer, I felt a growing sense of responsibility. The chief's words echoed in my mind, reminding me that I had been chosen to offer guidance and wisdom to the great king. I knew that my words could potentially change the course of history, and I felt the gravity of the situation settling upon my shoulders.

"You will need to be visible here Mike", said Ceres, "and remember, all you can do is offer advice. The King will ultimately make any decision based on his intentions – not yours. I will remain invisible, but fear not, I will be beside you at all times."

As we entered the building, we found King Alfred sitting upon his throne, deep in thought. His brow was furrowed, and his eyes held a distant look, as if he were grappling with an immense burden. I approached him slowly, my heart filled with compassion for the difficult decision he faced.

"Great King Alfred," I began, my voice soft but clear, "I come to you as a friend and a guide. I know the weight of the choice that lies before you, and I understand the fear and uncertainty that must be in your heart."

King Alfred looked up, his eyes meeting mine with a mixture of surprise and curiosity. "Who are you, stranger? And how do you know of the matters that trouble me?"

I smiled gently, "I am a traveller from a distant land, sent here to offer you counsel in your time of need. I have seen the love and devotion your people have for you, and I know that your decision will shape the future of your kingdom and the world beyond."

As I spoke, I could see the tension in King Alfred's face begin to ease, replaced by a glimmer of hope. "Tell me, wise traveller, what would you have me do? Should I lead my men into battle against the Danes, risking countless lives, or should I seek a path of peace, even if it means sacrificing my pride?"

I placed a hand on King Alfred's shoulder, my touch a gesture of comfort and support. "Your Majesty, true strength lies not in the might of arms, but in the power of compassion and understanding. Your people look to you for guidance and protection, and they will follow you, no matter the path you choose. But I believe that seeking peace, even in the face of great adversity, is the mark of a truly great leader."

King Alfred nodded slowly, his eyes shining with a newfound determination. "You speak with wisdom, traveller. I have always believed that a king's duty is to his people, and that sometimes, the bravest choice is the one that seeks to avoid bloodshed. I will send emissaries to the Danes, offering a hand of friendship and a chance for peace. It will not be an easy path, but it is the right one."

I felt a surge of pride and relief wash over me, knowing that my words had made a difference. I turned and saw Ceres as a misty glow standing behind me. He was smiling at me with approval, and together, we watched as King Alfred called for his advisors and began to plan for a new era of peace and prosperity.

As we left the grand building and made our way back through the village, I couldn't help but feel a deep sense of connection to the people around us. Though our time here was brief, I knew that the choices made on this day would ripple through history, shaping the lives of generations to come. And I felt honoured to have played a small part in guiding King Alfred towards a path of empathy, compassion, and lasting peace, but then, it would have happened anyway – such is destiny!

Ceres smiled at me and said, "We are now ready for our next journey through time. This time, we will explore the Enigma Stone."

"What and where is the Enigma Stone, Ceres?" I asked.

"The Enigma Stone is a legendary crystal born from the chaotic seas of Nu, the place of my birth," Ceres explained.

"This stone holds extraordinary powers, granting those who gaze into it visions of the past, present, and future. It provides access to the knowledge of all things, bridging the realms of reality and non-reality."

"The Enigma Stone's connection to me is profound," Ceres continued.

"It was attached to my embryo within the egg and has remained with me for time immemorial. Positioned behind my left ear, it is an integral part of me, symbolising the deep bond between my energetic self and the crystal."

"But the Enigma Stone is more than just a window into time," Ceres added.

"It can be used to uncover hidden truths, solve complex problems, and gain insights into the mysteries of the universe. It can guide decisions, inspire creativity, and even heal emotional wounds. However, only those deemed worthy, the 'chosen ones,' are permitted to look into the Enigma Stone, suggesting its powers are not meant for everyone. But because you are with me, you are the 'chosen one,' and I can allow you to look into it."

"To look into the Enigma Stone, we must embark on a journey to a remote part of the cosmos, where a crystal-lined cave awaits. This sacred space amplifies the stone's mystical properties, providing the perfect environment for the experience."

"Climb onto my back, close your eyes, and count down from 10. When you open your eyes, we will be in the 9th dimension of the Cosmos, and in a very special cave that only I know the existence of."

I did as Ceres said, somewhat nervous yet excited, and started to count, "10, 9, 8, 7…"

As we enter the cave, Ceres entered a meditative state, aligning his energies to facilitate the connection between me and the stone. Reaching behind his left ear, I saw a purple glowing area and placed my hands on it. Then I saw it in all its majesty. Upon gazing into the Enigma Stone, I was overwhelmed by a profound sense of awe and wonder. Visions of the past, present, and future unfolded before me, revealing hidden truths and insights into the universe's mysteries, some I understood, some I didn't. This experience completely altered my perception of reality and non-reality, and I was sure this would guide my future decisions and inspiring creativity. The knowledge that flowed from this stone seemed to be offering me solutions to complex problems and left me with a deep sense of responsibility and enlightenment.

I asked one question: "where to next?"

Then a huge image on the side of the cave showing a series of movie clips appeared, it looked hot and sandy…

CHAPTER TEN

Communication

KNIGHTS TEMPLAR AND THE CRUSADES 1192 AD

The images continued to flicker above my head, until one appeared, frozen, and a phrase materialised which simply said, 'place your hand here'. I looked nervously at Ceres, and he just nodded as if to say, 'go ahead, do it'.

As I put my right hand to the cave wall, I noticed that my clothes were changing. I now had a scarlet red cloak with a small white cross over my heart, a chain mail tunic underneath, brown stockings and tough leather shoes.

Ceres laughed and said, "looks like you are a squire in service of a knight, and judging from the red and white cloak, I would say you are in service of a Knight Templar and perhaps we are going to what you called, the Holy Land, during one of the many Crusades that the Christians waged war on the Muslims. This will be interesting."

"Oh, and by the way, as with your last encounter, you will be seen and heard, so careful what you say and do. Never fear though, I will be with you, although I will be invisible to all around, except you."

As I started to put my hand onto the cave wall, it seemed to sink straight through the hard rock exterior. A swirling vortex of iridescent colors pulsated with an otherworldly glow. The air crackled with energy, and as I stepped closer, a tingling sensation enveloped my skin. The portal's hues shifted from electric blues to fiery oranges, casting eerie reflections on the damp walls around me. Entering felt like wading through viscous liquid; time appeared to slow, and each of my heartbeats echoed like thunder. My surroundings started to blur into a kaleidoscope of light and sound, stretching and twisting. A rush of warmth flooded my senses as the cave around me dissolved, depositing me in a future world bathed in golden sunlight.

Upon emerging from the time portal, I found myself amidst the bustling encampment of what appeared to be a Crusader army.

The air was thick with the scent of sweat and leather, mingling with the aroma of cooking fires. Tents of varied colours and sizes stretched across the landscape, their banners flapping in the warm breeze. The camp was alive with activity: knights in shining armour tending to their horses, while foot soldiers were sharpening weapons and repairing gear. The sound of clashing swords from training sessions filled the air, as did the rhythmic chant of prayers from a nearby chapel tent.

Looking around, I decided that the best place to go first was to the chapel tent – at least that was probably safe! I hesitated at the tent opening, wondering what I might find on the other side and how I would be treated. But then again, I assumed that I was clothed correctly, so I shouldn't be that odd a figure. Before I could enter, a person, dressed just like me came stumbling out with a makeshift wooden cross in his hand. He looked at me and said, "Ah Roger, I am glad to see you have made the time to rejoice in God's message. We are going to cause havoc amongst those Muslim swine tomorrow." And without a second glance or delay for my reply, he was gone.

So, I was a 'Roger'. Roger who I wondered, and where from?

The smell of incense and a gentle humming of repeated prayer from within stirred me into action as I pulled back the tent flap and stepped inside.

It was a lot larger inside than I had imagined. The interior was packed with monks, serfs, squires, and knights all inside this unique and spiritually charged environment. The chapel tent itself was a large structure made of sturdy fabric, and adorned with Christian symbols such as crosses and the oval sign of peace. It was definitely spacious enough to accommodate around 50 persons I guessed.

The interior was dimly lit, primarily with candles placed strategically around the space. And as I looked on, this soft lighting created a solemn atmosphere which was conducive to prayer and reflection.

I think I had entered in the middle of a service as the ethereal sounds of Gregorian chants being sung by a cohort of monks was both simple in its melody and spiritual depth, and resonated throughout the tent, creating an atmosphere of reverence and contemplation.

I looked around and could see that there was a 'pecking order' in the attendees. Serfs wearing simple tunics, were at the back closest to the entrance and in front of them were what I assumed were squires dressed like me and at the front, half a dozen knights in elaborate attire, with white cloaks and huge red crosses covering their chests. They were all kneeling in rows and participating in the prayers and hymns.

Some of the monks were also performing rituals such as blessing the individuals in the congregation with holy water from a chalice with the sign of the cross. As a monk came towards me, I hurriedly got to my knees.

"Kneel my son" said the monk, whereupon I immediately did so. He muttered a Latin verse of some sort and made a gesture of the cross on my forehead. Smiling, he said "be not afraid of what the morrow brings as you have God with you my son," and moved onto the next man.

I decided to get out of this chapel tent as quickly as possible. As I stepped outside, it suddenly struck me that I was, in all probability, going into a battle tomorrow, with no idea who I was a squire to, how to help him prepare, where to go and even a simple thing like how to draw a sword!

The weight of my predicament pressed heavily on my chest as I wandered aimlessly through the encampment, my mind racing with questions. Who was I supposed to serve? What role did I have to play in this unfolding drama? The distant clang of swords and the murmur of voices brought me back to the present. I needed answers, and fast.

A voice whispered in my ear. It was Ceres. "Don't be worried Mike. Just let the events unfold in front of you. I think you will be surprised at what is about to happen. Be strong."

As I moved through the camp, I noticed a group of knights gathered around a central fire, their voices low but intense. Among them stood a figure who exuded authority - a man clad in ornate armour with a lion emblazoned on his chest. Richard the Lionheart! His piercing gaze swept over the camp as he addressed his men, his words sharp and commanding. Even from a distance, it was clear that this was a leader who inspired both fear and loyalty.

Not far from this scene, another figure caught my eye - a man dressed in flowing robes, seated cross-legged under a makeshift canopy. His demeanor was calm, almost serene, as he conversed with a small group of followers. This must have been Saladin. Though separated by distance and ideology, there was an undeniable similarity between the two leaders: both were men of immense charisma and conviction, yet their approaches to leadership seemed worlds apart.

Saladin was clearly here in the camp of his supposed enemy at Richard's request and protection. Who would have believed it?

It struck me then how pivotal communication would be in shaping the events to come. These two titans of history - Richard the Lionheart and Saladin - were not just warriors but negotiators, each wielding words as skillfully as they did swords. Their ability to communicate across cultural and religious divides would determine not only the fate of their armies but also the legacy of this Crusade.

I realised that my role here might not be to fight but to observe and learn. What could these two leaders teach me about bridging divides? About finding common ground amidst conflict? The Crusades were a brutal clash of civilizations, yet even in the chaos, moments of understanding and respect had emerged - like Richard's admiration for Saladin's chivalry or Saladin's decision to send his personal physician to treat Richard during an illness.

As I continued through the camp, I resolved to pay close attention to how these leaders communicated - not just with their allies but also with their enemies. Perhaps there was a lesson here for all of us: that even in the darkest times, dialogue could be a beacon of hope.

As I stood there, lost in thought, a hand clamped down on my shoulder. I spun around to see a tall, broad-shouldered man with a weathered face and piercing blue eyes. His chainmail glinted in the firelight, and the white cross on his surcoat marked him as a Knight Templar. "There you are, Roger," he said gruffly. "Daydreaming again, are we? Come, there's much to be done before dawn."

I nodded mutely, still unsure of who this man was or what my duties entailed. He didn't seem to notice my hesitation as he strode off toward a row of tents, gesturing for me to follow.

"Sir Baldwin will need his armour polished and his sword sharpened," he continued without looking back. "And make sure his horse is ready - he won't tolerate any delays tomorrow."

So, Sir Baldwin was my knight. At least now I had a name, though it did little to ease the knot of anxiety tightening in my chest. As we approached one of the larger tents, the man - who I assumed was another squire - turned to me with a smirk. "You're lucky, you know," he said.

"Sir Baldwin may be demanding, but he's fair. Better than serving some of the others." His tone darkened slightly as he added, "Not all knights live up to their oaths of chivalry."

Inside the tent, Sir Baldwin was seated on a wooden stool, examining a map spread out on a low table. He looked up as we entered, his sharp features framed by the flickering light of an oil lamp. "Ah, Roger," he said, his voice steady and authoritative. "Good. We have much to prepare for tomorrow's engagement." He gestured toward a pile of armour and weapons in the corner. "See to it."

I moved quickly to obey, though my hands trembled as I lifted the heavy breastplate from the pile. How was I supposed to clean and prepare this? I had no idea what I was doing, but I couldn't let that show - not now.

As I worked clumsily on the armour, Sir Baldwin began speaking again, this time addressing the other squire. "The Lionheart has summoned Saladin for another parley tonight," he said. "It seems they're still trying to negotiate terms before more blood is spilled." His tone was neutral, but there was a hint of curiosity in his eyes as he added, "Strange times we live in, when kings and sultans speak as equals."

The other squire shrugged. "Better they talk than fight," he said simply.

I listened intently as they continued their conversation, piecing together fragments of information about the upcoming battle and the uneasy truce that hung over the camp like a storm cloud. It was clear that both Richard and Saladin were men who understood the cost of war - not just in lives but in the toll it took on their people and their lands.

As night fell and the camp quieted, I found myself drawn toward the edge of the encampment where Richard and Saladin were meeting under a guarded pavilion. From a distance, I could see their silhouettes illuminated by torchlight: Richard's towering frame clad in gleaming armor and Saladin's robed figure seated with an air of calm dignity.

Though I couldn't hear their words, the sight of these two leaders - so different yet so alike - left an indelible impression on me. Here were two men who could have easily chosen hatred and destruction but instead sought understanding and compromise.

Ceres' voice echoed softly in my mind once more: "Pay attention, Mike. This is why you're here."

For all their differences - for all the bloodshed that had brought them to this moment - Richard and Saladin were proving that even amidst war, communication could be a bridge rather than a barrier. And perhaps that was the greatest lesson of all: that true strength lay not in wielding power but in knowing when to lay it down for the sake of peace.

As I turned back toward Sir Baldwin's tent, my resolve hardened. Whatever role I was meant to play here - whether as an observer or something more - I would do my best to learn from these extraordinary men and carry their lessons forward into my own time.

The camp was quieter now, the hum of activity reduced to the occasional clink of armour or the soft murmur of voices. The stars above shone brilliantly, their light casting a silver glow over the sprawling encampment.

As I approached Sir Baldwin's tent, I noticed him standing just outside, his arms crossed and his expression contemplative. He seemed lost in thought, his gaze fixed on the distant pavilion where Richard and Saladin continued their parley.

"Roger," he said without turning, his voice cutting through the stillness. "Do you know why we fight?" I hesitated, unsure how to respond. Was this a rhetorical question? A test? "For God and for the Holy Land," I replied cautiously, echoing what I assumed was the standard answer.

Sir Baldwin turned to face me, his eyes searching mine as if trying to gauge the sincerity of my words. "That's what they tell us," he said after a moment, his tone softer now. "But battles are rarely so simple. Faith may guide us, but ambition and pride often lead us astray."

His words surprised me. Here was a knight - a man sworn to defend Christendom - speaking with a level of introspection I hadn't expected. "Do you think this war can end with peace?" I asked tentatively. He sighed, running a hand through his graying hair. "If men like Richard and Saladin can find common ground, perhaps there's hope. But peace is fragile, Roger. It requires more courage than war."

His words lingered in my mind as I returned to my duties, polishing his armour with renewed determination. Sir Baldwin's perspective added another layer to what I was beginning to understand about this place and time. The Crusades were not just a clash of swords but a collision of ideals - faith against faith, culture against culture, leader against leader.

Later that night, as I lay on a rough cot in the corner of the tent, sleep eluded me. My mind kept drifting back to the image of Richard and Saladin under that pavilion, two giants of history locked in conversation rather than combat. What were they saying to each other? Were they discussing terms of surrender? A temporary truce? Or something deeper - an acknowledgment of their shared humanity despite their differences?

Ceres' voice broke through my thoughts once again. "You're beginning to see it now, aren't you?" he said softly. "The threads that connect us all."

I sat up abruptly, glancing around the darkened tent to ensure no one else could hear him. "What do you mean?" I whispered. "This moment," Ceres continued, "is more than just a meeting between two leaders. It's a reminder that even in times of division and conflict, there is always a chance for understanding. Richard and Saladin are showing you that strength is not just about dominance - it's about restraint, about knowing when to listen instead of speaking."

I nodded slowly, his words resonating with what I had witnessed so far. Perhaps my purpose here wasn't to change history but to learn from it - to carry these lessons back with me and apply them in my own time.

The next morning came too quickly, the camp stirring to life as dawn painted the horizon in hues of gold and crimson. The air was thick with anticipation; knights donned their armour while squires hurriedly prepared weapons and horses. Yet amidst the chaos, there was an undercurrent of uncertainty - whispers that the parley between Richard and Saladin had not yet concluded.

As Sir Baldwin mounted his horse and prepared for whatever lay ahead, he glanced down at me with an expression that was almost fatherly. "Stay close today," he said firmly. "And remember what we spoke about last night." I nodded, gripping the reins of his second horse tightly as we joined the procession heading toward the battlefield - or perhaps toward peace.

The tension was palpable as we approached the front lines where banners fluttered in the breeze and soldiers stood ready for orders. But then something unexpected happened: a messenger rode out from Richard's camp toward Saladin's forces bearing a white flag.

A hush fell over both armies as everyone watched with bated breath. The messenger stopped midway between the two camps and unfurled a scroll, his voice carrying across the field as he read aloud terms for an armistice. I glanced at Sir Baldwin, whose expression was unreadable. "This isn't over," he muttered under his breath. "But perhaps it's a start."

And in that moment, as both sides hesitated before lowering their weapons ever so slightly, I realised that history wasn't just shaped by battles won or lost - it was shaped by moments like this: moments where communication triumphed over conflict and dialogue opened doors that swords could not. This was why I was here - to witness not just war but the fragile seeds of peace being sown amidst its chaos. And as we turned back toward camp under orders to stand down for now, I felt a glimmer of hope that even in humanity's darkest hours, light could still break through.

It was abundantly clear to me that the overwhelming reason for me to be here was about what I had seen in my 'dream' of the oak tree and its 7 tunnels – it was clearly important for me to understand the different elements of this to carry forward into my 'normal' life back in the 21st century.

This is what I was picking up.

Communication is the exchange of ideas, thoughts, and information through speaking, writing, or using some other medium. It is a fundamental process that is essential to human interaction and the functioning of society.

Effective communication involves both the sender and the receiver of the message being able to understand and interpret the information being conveyed. It also involves being able to effectively express oneself and being open to hearing and considering the perspectives of others.

There are different types of communication, including verbal communication, which involves speaking and listening, and nonverbal communication, which involves body language, gestures, and facial expressions.

Effective communication is important in many aspects of life, including relationships, education, and the workplace. It can help to build trust, resolve conflicts, and improve understanding and cooperation. There are many skills that can help to improve communication, including active listening, being clear and concise, and being open to feedback.

I hope I was correct - it certainly felt correct.

CHAPTER ELEVEN

Spirit

ENGLISH CIVIL WAR (ROYALISTS), THE STORMING OF BRISTOL 1643 AD

Mike and Ceres stood amidst this parley between Crusaders and Muslim warriors. Mike felt a surge of emotion rise within him. This moment - this exchange - was exactly what Ceres had been trying to show him throughout their journey. Communication was not just an act; it was an act of courage. To speak to someone who might wish you harm required vulnerability and trust. It required seeing beyond the armour and weapons to recognise the humanity in another.

Mike, still grappling with the enormity of their journey through time, glanced at Ceres, the majestic dragon who had become his guide through these epochs of human emotion. Ceres's shimmering malachite scales caught the sunlight as he extended his clawed hand - or rather, talon - toward Mike.

"It is time," Ceres said, his voice resonating like a deep bell. "The next step in your journey awaits."

Mike hesitated. "Where now? And what am I supposed to learn this time?"

Ceres's eyes, deep pools of ancient wisdom, softened.

"We are standing in front of the far right root tunnel. We go to seventeenth century, to 1643 in fact, to the English Civil War. There you will witness the storming of Bristol - a moment charged with the raw essence of spirit. You will see it in those who fight against overwhelming odds, in their defiance, and in their unwavering belief in their cause. But first, we must travel."

Before Mike could respond, Ceres unfurled the amulet from his talon. It shimmered with an otherworldly glow, its surface etched with intricate runes that seemed to shift and dance as if alive.

"This amulet," Ceres explained, "is our passage. Here, take it and hold onto it tightly and focus on where we must go."

There was strange writing or runes etched on the amulet.

"What does this say, Ceres?"

Before Ceres could say, the gentle voice of Solarys answered.

"Ah, it says "Time bends, but truth endures eternally."

"This reflects the idea that while time and circumstances may shift, distort, or alter perceptions, truth remains constant and unchanging. Lies and falsehoods may dominate momentarily, but they are fleeting. Truth, by its nature, transcends time, standing as a reliable and eternal foundation for trust and understanding."

"So, an overall message for both of you is to speak your truth, knowing that it is the truth. Come on now, we must go."

Mike took a deep breath and grasped the amulet. The moment his fingers touched its surface, a surge of energy coursed through him.

The amulet seemed to activate, and the world around Mike dissolved into a mesmerising vortex of light and sound. This vortex was rather like a kaleidoscope, where fragments of history flashed before his eyes in rapid succession. These images were not random but appeared to represent significant moments or eras in human history, suggesting that Mike was being immersed in the continuum of time itself.

The sensory overload of the vortex - its dazzling lights and resonant sounds - created an otherworldly atmosphere, emphasising to Mike that he was leaving behind the physical constraints of his present reality. This transition was not just visual or auditory; it was deeply visceral, as though Mike's entire being was being pulled through the fabric of time.

The amulet was definitely acting as a bridge between dimensions, enabling Mike to traverse time in a way that felt both mystical and profoundly personal. This whole feeling highlighted the themes of transformation, connection to universal forces, and the interplay between past, present, and future.

When the whirlwind subsided, Mike found himself standing on a grassy hill overlooking a sprawling city encircled by fortifications. The air was heavy with tension; distant cannon fire echoed across the landscape. Smoke curled into the sky from various points within the city walls. It was Bristol in 1643.

Ceres stood beside him, now in a human form to avoid drawing undue attention with his bulk moving bushes, trees and even the ground he would walk on. His piercing blue eyes remained unchanged, a reminder of his true nature.

"Bristol," Ceres said simply. "The Royalists are about to storm it."

Mike scanned the scene below. Royalist forces were assembling - musketeers and pikemen readying themselves for battle under the command of Prince Rupert. The Parliamentarian defenders manned their posts along the city walls, their faces grim but resolute.

"Why here?" Mike asked.

"Because this is where you will understand what it means to embody spirit," Ceres replied. "Look closely at these men and women - both attackers and defenders. They fight not just for survival but for ideals greater than themselves."

As they descended toward the outskirts of the Royalist camp, Mike could feel the charged atmosphere - the mix of fear, determination, and hope that permeated the air.

The Royalist Camp

The Royalist camp was a hive of activity. Soldiers sharpened swords and loaded muskets while officers barked orders. Among them was Prince Rupert himself - a tall figure exuding confidence and authority despite the enormity of the task ahead.

Ceres guided Mike toward a group of Cornish foot soldiers seated around a small fire. Their faces were weathered, their uniforms patched and worn. Yet there was a spark in their eyes - a fierce determination that belied their exhaustion.

One soldier, a young man barely out of his teens, spoke passionately to his comrades. "We may be outnumbered and outgunned," he said, "but we fight for our king! For our land! For our families! If we fall here today, let it be known that we fell with honour."

Mike felt a lump rise in his throat as he listened. These men knew the odds were against them; they had seen comrades fall in previous battles. Yet they pressed on - not because they were forced to but because they believed in something greater than themselves.

"This," Ceres whispered to Mike, "is spirit. It is not about victory or defeat - it is about standing firm in the face of adversity."

The Assault on Bristol

As dawn broke on July 26th, 1643, the Royalists launched their assault on Bristol's fortifications. Cannon fire thundered across the battlefield as soldiers charged toward the city walls under heavy fire from Parliamentarian defenders.

Mike found himself swept up in the chaos, observing both sides with growing admiration. He saw Royalist soldiers using carts laden with faggots to fill ditches while others scaled ladders under a hail of musket balls. On the walls above, Parliamentarian defenders fought valiantly to repel them - hurling stones and firing down into the melee below.

Amidst this chaos, Mike spotted moments that epitomised spirit. A Royalist officer rallied his men after their initial charge faltered; his voice rang out above the din: "Hold fast! For king and country!" Inspired by his courage, they surged forward once more.

On another part of the battlefield, a Parliamentarian woman - likely a civilian - stood atop the walls alongside her husband and son. She hurled stones at advancing Royalists with fierce determination despite her obvious fear.

"These are ordinary people doing extraordinary things," Mike said aloud.

Ceres nodded solemnly beside him. "Indeed. This is what I wanted you to see - that spirit transcends rank or station. It resides in anyone who dares to stand for what they believe in."

As Mike and Ceres observed the unfolding siege, an unusual occurrence caught their attention. Among the Royalist forces, a group of soldiers carried what appeared to be an ancient wooden chest, carefully protected even in the heat of battle.

The chest bore strange markings that seemed to shimmer in the evening light.

"What do you make of that?" Mike asked, pointing to the mysterious container.

Ceres's eyes narrowed as he studied the chest. "That," he said slowly, "is no ordinary war treasure. Those markings... they're Celtic in origin, far older than this conflict."

As they watched, the soldiers deposited the chest in a makeshift command tent where Prince Rupert stood examining maps of Bristol's defences.

The prince's reaction to the chest's arrival was peculiar - he dismissed all but his most trusted advisors and ordered the tent sealed.

"There's more to this than meets the eye," Ceres murmured.

"The chest contains something of great spiritual significance. Look closely at how the markings pulse with energy - they're responding to the violence around them."

Mike strained his eyes and indeed saw a faint bluish glow emanating from the chest's seams. "What could it be?"

"Let's find out," Ceres replied. "Remember, we're invisible to them. We can observe without being detected."

They approached the command tent, passing through its canvas walls as if they were mist. Inside, Prince Rupert and three advisors stood around the chest, speaking in hushed tones.

"The prophecy speaks true," one advisor said, his fingers tracing the Celtic symbols. "When the city falls, the spirit stone must be placed at the highest point of Bristol's defences before sunset. Only then will the kingdom's future be secured."

Mike glanced at Ceres, who had grown very still. The dragon's eyes glowed with recognition.

"The spirit stone," Ceres whispered to Mike. "I haven't seen one in centuries. They were created by ancient druids to channel the collective spirit of a people. This one must have been discovered in Cornwall and brought here deliberately."

"But why Bristol? Why now?" Mike asked.

"Because Bristol sits at the convergence of powerful ley lines - channels of spiritual energy that crisscross your land. The Royalists believe that by placing the stone at the right point during a moment of great spiritual significance - like this battle - they can harness its power to influence the outcome of the entire war."

Mike watched as Prince Rupert carefully opened the chest. Inside lay a crystalline stone about the size of a man's fist, swirling with colours that seemed to respond to the emotions in the air - flashing red with anger, deep blue with determination, gold with hope.

"The stone absorbs and amplifies the spiritual energy of those around it," Ceres explained. "In the wrong hands, it could be used to manipulate the spirits of men, bend their will to a cause. But it's true purpose was to unite, not divide."

As they observed, Prince Rupert's expression grew troubled. "The stone grows dim," he said to his advisors. "Its power wanes. Why?"

Mike looked questioningly at Ceres, who nodded gravely. "The stone senses the discord in the land. It was created to channel the unified spirit of a people, but this war has torn the spirit of England in two. Brother against brother, father against son - such division weakens its power."

"Can anything be done?" Mike asked.

"That's why we're here," Ceres replied. "Watch and learn. The mystery of the spirit stone holds a lesson about the true nature of power and unity."

As the day wore on and the battle raged, Mike and Ceres witnessed Prince Rupert's growing frustration. The stone's light continued to fade despite the Royalists' advances. Even when they succeeded in breaching Bristol's defences, the crystal remained dim.

"He doesn't understand," Ceres said. "The stone's power cannot be seized through force. It must be earned through unity of spirit."

As sunset approached, Prince Rupert ordered the stone to be carried to Bristol's highest tower. Mike and Ceres followed the procession through the chaos of the captured city. Everywhere they looked, they saw the cost of division - wounded soldiers from both sides, frightened civilians, buildings in flames.

At the tower's summit, Prince Rupert raised the stone high, expecting it to blaze with power. Instead, it grew darker still.

"Now watch," Ceres said softly. "Watch what happens when true spirit manifests."

Below them, something remarkable began to occur. A group of Royalist soldiers, instead of pursuing their victory, had stopped to help wounded Parliamentarian defenders. A civilian woman offered water to exhausted fighters from both sides. Small acts of compassion bloomed amid the devastation.

The stone responded instantly, pulsing with a pure white light that illuminated the entire tower.

"You see?" Ceres said to Mike.

"The stone's true power lies not in victory over others, but in victory over our own darker natures. When people remember their shared humanity, even in the midst of conflict - that is true spirit."

Prince Rupert stared at the glowing stone in wonder, perhaps beginning to understand what they had known all along. He ordered his men to cease their pursuit of fleeing defenders and instead focus on helping the wounded and extinguishing fires.

"The mystery of the spirit stone wasn't really about the stone at all, was it?" Mike asked.

"No," Ceres smiled. "It was about understanding that spirit - true spirit - cannot be captured or controlled. It emerges naturally when people remember their connection to one another. That's what makes it so powerful, and so precious."

As night fell over Bristol, the spirit stone continued to glow, its light a beacon of hope in the darkness. Prince Rupert ordered it sealed away again, perhaps realising that its lesson was more valuable than its power.

"Remember this, Mike," Ceres said as they prepared to leave this moment in history. "In your time, as in all times, people will seek to control and divide. But true spirit - the kind that changes hearts and heals wounds - comes from remembering our shared humanity. That's the real magic, and it's within everyone's reach."

The stone's glow faded as they stepped back through time, but its lesson remained: that in the darkest moments, it is not conquest but compassion that reveals the true strength of the human spirit.

As they prepared to leave this tumultuous chapter behind, Mike felt a newfound respect for those who had fought at Bristol - on both sides of the conflict - and an understanding that spirit was not confined to any one moment or place but was an eternal force guiding humanity through its darkest hours.

With that thought lingering in his mind, he grasped the glowing amulet once more - and together with Ceres - vanished into another chapter of history yet to unfold…

CHAPTER TWELVE

Fire Breathing and Advanced Flight

At the Dragon Academy, we young dragons learned how to breathe fire through a combination of biological mastery, alchemical knowledge, and rigorous training. The process was rooted in both our innate physiology and our ability to harness external elements. Here's how we were taught this iconic skill.

It's an amazing fact Mike but we possess specialised organs that enabled us to produce and control fire. Drawing inspiration from natural phenomena like the bombardier beetle and spitting cobras, our biology is perfectly adapted for flame production:

Fire Production Systems

Chemical Reaction Chambers: Dragons had internal reservoirs where volatile chemicals were stored separately. When needed, these chemicals were mixed in a reaction chamber, creating an exothermic reaction that produced heat and flame.

Ignition Mechanisms: Dragons could generate sparks to ignite their flames. This might involve flint-like scales or mineral coatings on their teeth, which created sparks when struck together.

Fuel Sources: Their digestive systems produced flammable gases like methane or stored combustible oils derived from their carnivorous diets. These fuels were expelled in controlled bursts to sustain the flame.

Training at the Academy

The Academy provided structured training to help dragons refine their fire-breathing abilities:

Control and Precision: Young dragons practiced controlling the intensity and direction of their flames in specialized chambers designed to withstand heat and fire.

Chemical Balancing: They learned how to regulate the mixing of volatile substances within their bodies to avoid misfires or self-harm.

Ignition Techniques: Dragons were taught how to use their natural spark-generating mechanisms effectively, ensuring reliable ignition without damaging themselves.

Environmental Adaptation: Training included exercises in various environments to teach dragons how to adapt their fire-breathing based on atmospheric conditions.

Purpose of Fire-Breathing

Beyond combat or hunting, dragons were taught the ecological and dimensional significance of their flames:

Clearing overgrown landscapes for new growth.

Providing warmth or light in dark or cold dimensions.

Defending against threats while maintaining balance across realms.

Learning to Fly

The art of flight was perhaps our most cherished skill, taught alongside fire-breathing from our earliest days at the Academy. Young dragons began their journey on the Windward Cliffs, where thermal currents provided natural lift for our first tentative wing-beats. Our instructors taught us that true flight wasn't just about raw strength—it was about understanding the wind, reading air currents, and mastering our own bodies.

The learning process started with gliding exercises, allowing young dragons to develop a feel for their wings and tail rudders. We would spend hours studying the wing structures of various birds and analyzing how our own anatomy differed. Our massive wing membranes required different techniques than the feathered wings of birds, and we learned to use our tail fins for precise directional control.

Advanced Aerial Manoeuvres and Their Dangers

As we progressed, we learned increasingly complex aerial manoeuvres, each carrying its own risks. The infamous "Thunder Roll"—a high-speed vertical climb followed by a backwards rotation—claimed many scales before mastery. The greatest danger came from what our instructors called "velocity lock," where a dragon's momentum could override their ability to change direction.

High-speed flight brought unique challenges. At extreme velocities, the pressure on our wings could tear the membranes if we didn't maintain perfect form. The "sonic barrier," as we called it, required special training to navigate. Many young dragons learned the hard way that breaking the sound barrier without proper preparation could result in temporary disorientation or even unconsciousness.

The Art of Stealth Flight

Perhaps our most sophisticated skill was the art of concealment during flight. Dragons possessed a remarkable ability to blend with their surroundings through a combination of biological and magical adaptations. Our scales contained specialised crystals that could refract light, creating a chameleon-like effect that made us nearly invisible against the sky. These microscopic structures, arranged in overlapping patterns along our flanks and wings, worked in concert with ancient magics to bend light around our forms.

We learned to fly using thermal layers to mask our heat signatures, and to time our movements with cloud patterns to remain undetected. The Academy taught us to use natural phenomena like sun glare and weather conditions to our advantage. Rising before dawn, we would practice gliding through morning mist, our bodies ghosting through layers of fog until we could navigate by feel alone. Veterans spoke of how young dragons often failed to grasp the subtleties of thermal masking - it wasn't enough to simply soar through warm air currents. One had to learn to regulate internal body temperature, carefully modulating our natural fire to prevent telltale heat plumes from rising above the clouds.

Special attention was paid to reducing our acoustic signature - the distinctive whoosh of dragon wings could carry for miles if not properly controlled. We spent countless hours perfecting the art of silent flight, learning to adjust the angle of our wing membranes to minimise air disturbance. The most skilled among us could alter the very flexibility of our wing tissue, softening it during downstrokes to muffle the sound of displaced air. The masters dragons taught us to recognise the acoustic properties of different atmospheres - humid air carried sound differently than dry, cold air differently than warm. On moonless nights, we would practice what the Academy called "ghost gliding," moving through darkness with such precision that not even the keenest-eared owl could detect our passage.

The crystalline scales that aided our visual camouflage served another purpose in stealth flight. When properly aligned through careful muscle control, they could dampen magical emanations that might otherwise give away our position to sensitive practitioners. This technique, known as "aetheric dampening," was considered essential for any dragon who wished to move undetected through areas heavy with magical activity. The most accomplished stealth flyers could even use their scales to absorb and redirect ambient magical energy, creating false signatures that would lead observers to look in entirely wrong directions.

Yet perhaps the most challenging aspect of stealth flight was learning to coordinate these various techniques simultaneously. A single lapse in concentration could reveal our presence - a moment of excitement causing a thermal spike, a wingbeat slightly too forceful producing an audible whisper, or a brief misalignment of scales creating a telltale glimmer. The Academy's final tests would often last for days, requiring students to maintain perfect stealth while navigating complex courses under varying conditions. Those who mastered these skills earned the coveted title of Shadowwing, though many of us would spend lifetimes perfecting the art of moving unseen through the ever-watching skies.

The Legend of Ceres

Let me show you a snippet of dragon history through the Academy Book of Heroes. This is kept in the Chamber of Heat and can only be read by permission of the Keeper of the book which happens to be Solarys!

No chapter on dragon flight would be complete without mentioning Ceres, whose aerial prowess became legendary among our kind. Stories tell of his mastery of the "Silent Glide," a technique that allowed him to soar for days without a single wing beat. He was the first to perfect the "Starfall Manoeuvre," diving from the stratosphere at speeds that made him appear as nothing more than a shooting star to ground observers.

Ceres revolutionized our understanding of high-altitude flight, discovering wind patterns in the upper atmosphere that we now call "Ceres Streams." His most remarkable achievement came during the Great Storm of the Eastern Realms, where he guided a formation of young dragons through a category five hurricane, using the storm's own energy to power their flight. To this day, his techniques form the cornerstone of advanced flight training at the Academy.

Through years of practice and mentorship at the Dragon Academy, young dragons mastered fire-breathing as both a practical tool and a symbol of their power and responsibility. This skill, combined with our mastery of flight and stealth, became an integral part of our role as stewards of harmony across dimensions.

CHAPTER THIRTEEN

Perseverance

THE LONDON UNDERGROUND 1820 AD

The tunnel before Mike and Ceres glowed with an unusual purple hue, different from any they had encountered before.

As they approached, Solarys' amulet began to pulse with an answering light.

"This tunnel holds something special," Solarys' melodic voice echoed in their minds.

"Here you will witness not just perseverance but connect with an ancient force that embodies it."

Mike looked questioningly at Ceres, who nodded encouragingly.

"Solarys speaks of the Eternal Flame of Persistence - a cosmic force as old as time itself. Few humans have ever perceived it, though many have unconsciously drawn upon its power."

As they entered the tunnel, the purple light intensified. Mike felt a strange tingling sensation throughout his body, as if every cell was being energized by an otherworldly power.

"Close your eyes," Solarys instructed. "Feel the rhythm of perseverance that flows through all existence."

Mike did as instructed. Immediately, he was overwhelmed by visions - countless beings across time and space, pushing through seemingly insurmountable obstacles. He saw stars being born, straining against the void to ignite their cores. He witnessed mountains slowly rising from the earth over millions of years. He observed simple organisms evolving over eons, never giving up their drive to survive and adapt.

"The Eternal Flame burns in all things," Solarys explained. "But in humans, it can burn brightest of all - when they choose to fuel it."

When Mike opened his eyes, they were standing in London, 1820, deep beneath the city streets. The air was thick with coal dust and the sounds of picks striking rock echoed through the darkness. By the light of guttering lanterns, dozens of workers - men, women, and even children - laboured in the cramped tunnel. The scene shifted and flowed around them as Solarys guided them through different moments in the massive project's history.

"Watch them," Ceres indicated the workers, their faces streaked with grime. "These are the 'clay-kickers' - lying on their backs, using their feet to drive spades into the earth above them. The technique was invented out of desperate necessity when traditional mining methods proved too dangerous in London's unpredictable soil."

They watched as workers struggled with one of their greatest challenges - the treacherous layer of quicksand that lay beneath much of London.

"Here," Ceres explained, "they're using Brunel's revolutionary tunnelling shield - an iron framework divided into cells, each containing a worker who digs at the face while bricklayers behind them line the tunnel with concrete. It's revolutionary, but still incredibly dangerous."

Mike observed as workers battled against frequent flooding. The Thames above them was a constant threat, its waters seeking any weakness in their defences. In one section, they used massive steam-powered pumps working day and night to keep the water at bay. Despite their efforts, he witnessed several devastating breakthroughs where the river crashed through, filling tunnels in minutes.

The scene before them suddenly focused on a particular day - May 18th, 1827. Mike watched in horror as a massive crack appeared in the tunnel ceiling, followed by an ominous rumbling sound. The purple flame in the workers' chests flared brilliantly as they realized what was coming.

"Get out! The river's breaking through!" someone shouted.

But before most could react, the Thames crashed through the ceiling with devastating force. The torrent of water was horrifying - a solid wall of dark water carrying debris and mud, roaring into the tunnel like a furious beast.

"Watch," Ceres directed, as the scene unfolded. "Watch how the Eternal Flame manifests in crisis."

Through the chaos, Mike saw extraordinary acts of courage. A burly worker named James Beamish stayed behind, lifting smaller workers onto a scaffold above the rising water. The purple flame in his chest burned so bright it seemed to illuminate the tunnel around him. Even as the water reached his chest, he continued helping others to safety.

Above ground, the newly-formed London police force mobilized with remarkable speed. Sergeant William Peters, his own purple flame blazing, coordinated with local fire brigades and volunteers. They began lowering ropes and ladders into every shaft they could access.

"The flame burns differently in each person," Solarys observed, "but in moments like this, they unite into something greater."

Mike watched as firefighters from three different stations fought their way down flooded shafts, forming human chains to reach trapped workers. Local publicans and shopkeepers joined the effort, bringing blankets and brandy for those pulled from the freezing water.

A young police constable named Thomas Harris stripped off his heavy uniform and dived repeatedly into the flooded tunnel, guided only by the desperate sounds of trapped workers. The purple flame in his chest seemed to create a path through the murky water. On his third dive, he found two young boys clinging to a timber beam, nearly unconscious from the cold. Somehow, he managed to get both of them to safety.

But the most remarkable sight was Mary Combs, wife of one of the engineers, who organized a group of local women to form a second line of rescue. They created a system of pulleys using their washing lines, allowing rescuers to send down supplies and bring up survivors more quickly. The purple flame burned just as bright in these women as in any of the official rescuers.

As the rescue effort continued through the night, hundreds of Londoners came to help. Doctors set up emergency stations. Bakers brought hot food. Children ran messages between rescue teams. The Eternal Flame seemed to spread from person to person, growing stronger with each act of courage and kindness.

"This is what humans are capable of," Ceres said softly. "When the flame burns bright enough, it connects them, makes them stronger together than they ever could be alone."

In the end, though seven lives were lost, dozens more were saved by the extraordinary efforts of ordinary people who refused to give up. And remarkably, even as they pulled the last bodies out, others stepped forward to begin the work of repair. The Eternal Flame burned too bright to be quenched by even the Thames itself.

They moved to a different section where workers struggled with poisonous gases seeping from the earth. Men would take turns entering the most dangerous areas, working in short shifts until dizziness forced them to retreat. The purple flame in their chests seemed to flare brighter with each return to the deadly task.

"The challenges weren't just underground," Ceres added, as the scene shifted to the surface. They watched as residents protested the construction, fearful their homes would collapse into the tunnels below. Local businesses sued for compensation as streets were torn up and trade disrupted. Each setback required new solutions, new approaches, new reserves of determination.

The scene shifted again, and they found themselves in a more elegant setting - Queen Victoria's private chambers. The monarch stood over a detailed model of the underground system, her face thoughtful as Marc Brunel explained his vision.

"Her Majesty was initially skeptical," Solarys explained. "But she came to see this project as a testament to British ingenuity and determination. Watch."

The Queen moved through the actual tunnels now, amid crowds of cheering workers. The purple flame burned bright in her chest too as she spoke with labourers and engineers, coming to understand the true magnitude of their achievement.

"This project will stand as a monument," they heard her declare, "not just to British engineering, but to the indomitable spirit of our working people. Each brick, each beam, each foot of progress has been bought with their sweat and blood and unshakeable resolve."

They watched as families of workers gathered for the opening ceremony - mothers who had worked alongside their sons, wives who had nursed husbands through injuries only to see them return to the tunnels, children who had grown up carrying water and tools through the narrowest passages.

"The hardship was beyond measure," Ceres said. "They faced cave-ins that could strike without warning. Tunnels that could flood in seconds. Air so foul it could kill with a single breath. Wages that barely kept their families fed. Yet they persisted."

Mike watched a young boy, no more than ten, squeezing through a gap barely wider than his shoulders to reach a flooded section. The purple flame in his chest burned as bright as any adult's. "Some of the most dangerous work fell to the children," Solarys explained. "Their size made them invaluable for reaching difficult spaces. Many never lived to see the project completed."

Yet amid the hardship, Mike could see moments of triumph.

Workers celebrating as sections were completed. Engineers solving seemingly impossible problems with innovative solutions. Families gathering their meagre savings to buy shares in the project, believing in it so completely they would stake their futures on its success.

"Look there," Ceres directed Mike's attention to a group of workers standing proudly before a completed tunnel section.

"Every one of them was told this was impossible. That no one could tunnel under a river. That the whole thing would collapse. That they were fools to try. But the Eternal Flame burned in them too bright to be denied."

"The flame never wavers," Solarys added. "Through darkness, through danger, through endless setbacks - it keeps burning until the impossible becomes possible. These people didn't just build tunnels, they expanded the boundaries of what humanity thought was achievable."

As they prepared to leave, Mike took one last look at the workers. The purple fire still burned bright in all of them, a testament to the indomitable spirit that would eventually create not just a tunnel, but an entire underground world beneath London's streets. Their achievement would inspire similar projects across the globe, as other cities saw what perseverance could accomplish.

"Take this gift with you," Solarys said. "The ability to see the Flame in others, and to recognize it in yourself. Let it remind you that perseverance is not just a human virtue - it is a cosmic force, as fundamental as gravity or light."

Mike nodded, feeling the Flame kindle in his own heart. As they stepped back into the tunnel, he understood that he had witnessed more than just a historical moment - he had glimpsed one of the fundamental powers that shaped existence itself.

The tunnel's purple light began to fade, but the memory of the Eternal Flame remained with Mike - a new awareness of the unstoppable force that drove all progress, all evolution, all achievement. It was a lesson he would carry forward, not just in memory, but in the very fibre of his being.

"Ready for our next journey?" Ceres asked, his scales glimmering in the dimming light.

Mike touched the spot in his chest where he could still feel the Flame burning. "Ready," he replied, knowing that whatever challenges lay ahead, the fire of perseverance would help light the way.

CHAPTER FOURTEEN

Salvation

A s Mike stood in the ethereal cave for what he believed would be the last time, the weight of his extraordinary journey settled over him like a warm blanket. The tunnels that had led him through time and space were now sealed bar one, their ancient markings glowing faintly in the crystalline light. Only Ceres remained, his magnificent form casting dancing shadows on the cave walls.

"You've shown me so much," Mike said, his voice thick with emotion. "Tolerance from the Druids, love from the Vikings, communication from the Crusaders, spirit from the Civil War, and perseverance from the Underground builders. Each lesson more profound than the last."

"And what's more, Mike continued, "these are all lessons that have not been fairly portrayed by historians to us all through the ages. I remember being told at school that Columbus 'discovered' the New World, yet we saw Erik and his crew talking with Askook the Indigenous Chieftain, hundreds of years before. We were told so many things that actually never happened, but we never questioned. Now is the time for revelation!"

Ceres's eyes, deep pools of ancient wisdom, fixed upon Mike with gentle intensity. "And what have you learned from all of this, my friend?"

Mike closed his eyes, allowing the memories to wash over him.

"I've learned that humanity's greatest strength lies not in its differences, but in its shared experiences. The Druid chieftain Iseldir taught me that tolerance isn't just accepting others but understanding them. The Viking settlers showed me that love can bridge any divide. The Crusaders proved that even bitter enemies can find common ground through communication.

King Alfred showed considerable empathy, and the Civil War demonstrated how spirit can unite people in the darkest times. And those brave souls building the Underground showed me that perseverance can overcome any obstacle."

"But more than that," Mike continued, opening his eyes, "I've learned that these aren't just historical lessons – they're threads that weave through all of human existence. They're as relevant today as they were centuries ago."

Ceres nodded, his scales shimming with approval. "And what will you do with this knowledge?"

"I'll share it," Mike said firmly. "Not just the stories, but the understanding behind them. People need to know that we're all connected by these fundamental emotions and experiences. That the struggles and triumphs of our ancestors are our own. That the power to change the world lies in recognising our shared humanity."

A smile played across Ceres's magnificent features. "Then you have truly learned what I hoped to teach."

Mike stepped forward, reaching out to touch Ceres's warm scales one last time. "Will I ever see you again?"

The dragon's amulet, Solarys, suddenly pulsed with brilliant light. "The end of one journey is often the beginning of another," Solarys's voice echoed through the cave. "What you have learned is not meant to sit idle, but to grow and spread like ripples in a pond."

Ceres lowered his massive head until his eye was level with Mike's. "Look for me in the rushing wind," he said softly. "In the whisper of leaves, in the dance of flames, in the courage of those who stand up for what's right. I am not leaving you, Mike. I'm becoming part of your story – just as you have become part of mine."

The cave began to fade around them, the crystals dimming one by one. But before it disappeared completely, Ceres pressed something into Mike's hand – a single scale, gleaming with the colours of malachite.

"When you need guidance, hold this and remember," Ceres said, his voice growing distant. "Remember that every act of kindness, every moment of understanding, every bridge built between different peoples adds to the light in the world. That is your mission now – not just to remember, but to inspire others to see what you have seen."

The cave dissolved into mist leaving but one tunnel. Mike stepped forward, and almost immediately found himself back in the meditation room where his journey had begun. The scale in his hand glowed warmly, pulsing in time with his heartbeat.

Through the window, he could see the old oak tree in his garden, its leaves dancing in a sudden gust of wind.

Standing up, Mike walked to his desk and began to write. He would tell their story – not just his journey with Ceres, but the story of humanity's eternal struggle to understand itself. He would share the wisdom of Iseldir, the love of the Vikings, the spirit of the Civil War soldiers, and the perseverance of the Underground builders.

As he wrote, the scale beside him continued to pulse, and sometimes, in the quiet moments between words, he could have sworn he heard Ceres's voice on the wind, encouraging him onward. For this wasn't an ending at all, he realised. It was a beginning – the start of a new journey to share what he had learned with a world that desperately needed to remember its own humanity.

And somewhere, in the spaces between moments, in the rushing of the wind and the whisper of leaves, Ceres smiled.

For he knew that the real magic had never been in the time travel or the mystical caves, but in the simple truth that when humans truly understand their shared story, they can move mountains, bridge divides, and transform the world.

The next morning, as Mike sat beneath the old oak tree in his garden, a familiar warmth spread through his chest. The malachite scale in his pocket hummed with energy, and the rushing wind carried a whisper that sounded suspiciously like dragon's laughter. He smiled, knowing that his journey with Ceres wasn't over – it was just beginning in a different form.

For now, he understood that salvation wasn't about grand gestures or magical interventions. It was about the small moments of connection, the daily choices to understand rather than judge, to love rather than fear, to persevere rather than give up.

And as he watched the sun rise over his garden, Mike knew that somewhere, Ceres was watching too, ready to guide him on whatever adventures lay ahead.

After all, the best stories never really end – they just flow into new beginnings.

Six months later, Mike stood before a crowded auditorium, the malachite scale warm against his chest where it hung on a simple leather cord. His book, "The Rushing Wind: A Dragon's Lessons in Humanity," had touched something deep in people's hearts, spreading far beyond what he could have imagined.

But it wasn't the success that moved him – it was the stories that came after. Every day, his inbox filled with messages from readers who had found their own moments of connection, their own bridges to build.

A Muslim family and their Christian neighbours sharing meals during Ramadan. A corporate executive starting a mentorship program pairing elderly craftsmen with inner-city youth. A group of environmental activists and coal miners coming together to design sustainable futures for their community.

"The magic was always there," Mike began, his voice steady despite his racing heart. "Not in the dragon's cave or the time tunnels, but in the choices we make every day. In the moment we choose to listen instead of speak, to understand instead of judge, to reach out instead of pull away."

The scale pulsed gently, and Mike could have sworn he felt Ceres's presence in the subtle shift of air currents through the room. He smiled, remembering the dragon's words about being found in the rushing wind.

As he spoke, sharing stories from his journey, Mike noticed something extraordinary happening in the audience. People who had entered as strangers were turning to each other, sharing quiet words and knowing looks. The barriers that usually kept them apart – age, race, belief, status – seemed to dissolve in the face of these universal truths.

"But the most remarkable thing," Mike continued, "isn't what I learned in the past. It's what I see happening right here, right now. Every day, I witness people taking these ancient lessons and transforming them into modern bridges. You see, Ceres showed me the path, but you – all of you – are the ones walking it."

After the talk, as the audience filed out, an elderly woman approached Mike. Her eyes were bright with unshed tears, and in her hands, she clutched a worn photograph.

"My grandfather," she said softly, holding out the image, "was one of those Underground builders."

Mike's heart skipped a beat as he studied the sepia-toned photograph. The man in it stood proud despite his dirt-covered clothes, his eyes holding the same determined spirit he had witnessed in his journey.

"He never lived to see his work completed," she continued, "but he believed in it with every fibre of his being. When I read your book, about the perseverance of those builders... it was like hearing his voice again. Understanding, finally, what drove him to give everything for a future he would never see."

The scale warmed against Mike's chest, and a gentle breeze stirred the papers on the nearby table, carrying with it the faintest scent of malachite and ancient stone.

"Would you tell me more about him?" Mike asked, gesturing to a nearby bench.

As they sat together, their conversation drew others – a young student filming a documentary about urban development, a civil engineer working on sustainable housing projects, a community organiser fighting for immigrant rights.

Soon, they were all sharing stories, weaving together past and present, finding echoes of Iseldir's tolerance, the Vikings' love, the Crusaders' communication, the Civil War's spirit, and the Underground builders' perseverance in their own lives and work.

As the group talked, Mike felt the scale's warmth spread through his entire body. He understood now why Ceres had chosen to become part of the story rather than remain its guide. The dragon had known that true magic lies not in supernatural wonders, but in the moment when humans recognise themselves in each other's stories.

That evening, as Mike walked home through the city streets, he saw his journey reflected everywhere – in the diverse groups of people sharing meals at sidewalk cafes, in the community garden where elderly immigrants taught local children about plants from their homelands, in the street art that transformed messages of division into visions of unity.

The wind picked up, carrying fallen leaves in a spiralling dance around him. For just a moment, in the swirling patterns, Mike saw the distinct outline of a dragon's wing. He touched the scale at his chest and smiled, knowing that Ceres had been right. This wasn't just his story anymore – it had become part of the greater human narrative, a reminder that in every age, in every challenge, our salvation lies in our ability to see ourselves in each other.

And somewhere, in the spaces between heartbeats, in the pause between words, in the moment when understanding bridges the gap between strangers, Ceres's magic lived on, transforming the world one story at a time.

For in the end, the greatest magic of all is not in travelling through time, but in recognising that every moment offers us the chance to choose understanding over fear, connection over division, and love over indifference. These are the real tunnels through time – the choices that connect us to our shared humanity, past, present, and future.

And as Mike reached his garden, where the old oak tree stood sentinel against the darkening sky, he knew that his journey would continue as long as there were stories to share and bridges to build. For that was Ceres's true gift – not the magical moments in the cave, but the understanding that every one of us carries the power to transform the world, one act of connection at a time.

Suddenly, in the peace of the garden, Mike heard a whisper, "don't think for a moment that we haven't finished our journeying…"

Peace to all of you.

THE END

www.ingramcontent.com/pod-product-compliance
Lightning Source LLC
Chambersburg PA
CBHW071430300726
48976CB00004B/1287